Jane Austen

The Novels

Volume 2

Jane Austen

The Novels
Volume 2

ISBN/EAN: 9783337264369

Printed in Europe, USA, Canada, Australia, Japan

Cover: Foto ©Andreas Hilbeck / pixelio.de

More available books at **www.hansebooks.com**

THE NOVELS OF
JANE AUSTEN
WINCHESTER
EDITION
VOLUME
II

THE NOVELS OF
JANE AUSTEN

SENSE AND SENSIBILITY

VOLUME II

LONDON: GRANT RICHARDS

9 HENRIETTA STREET, W.C.

1898

Edinburgh : T. and A. Constable, Printers to Her Majesty

SENSE AND SENSIBILITY

II

SENSE AND SENSIBILITY

CHAPTER XXX

MRS. JENNINGS came immediately to their room on her return, and without waiting to have her request of admittance answered, opened the door and walked in with a look of real concern.

'How do you do, my dear?' said she, in a voice of great compassion, to Marianne, who turned away her face without attempting to answer.

'How is she, Miss Dashwood? Poor thing! she looks very bad. No wonder. Ay, it is but too true. He is to be married very soon—a good-for-nothing fellow! I have no patience with him. Mrs. Taylor told me of it half an hour ago, and she was told it by a particular friend of Miss Grey herself, else I am sure I should not have believed it; and I was almost ready to sink as it was. Well, said I, all I can say is, that if it is true, he has used a young lady of my acquaintance abominably ill, and I wish with all my soul his wife may plague his

2 A   1

heart out. And so I shall always say, my dear, you may depend on it. I have no notion of men's going on in this way; and if ever I meet him again, I will give him such a dressing as he has not had this many a day. But there is one comfort, my dear Miss Marianne : he is not the only young man in the world worth having ; and with your pretty face you will never want admirers. Well, poor thing ! I won't disturb her any longer, for she had better have her cry out at once and have done with it. The Parrys and Sandersons luckily are coming to-night, you know, and that will amuse her.'

She then went away, walking on tiptoe out of the room, as if she supposed her young friend's affliction could be increased by noise.

Marianne, to the surprise of her sister, determined on dining with them. Elinor even advised her against it. But 'no, she would go down ; she could bear it very well, and the bustle about her would be less.' Elinor, pleased to have her governed for a moment by such a motive, though believing it hardly possible that she could sit out the dinner, said no more ; and adjusting her dress for her as well as she could while Marianne still remained on the bed, was ready to assist her into the dining-room as soon as they were summoned to it.

When there, though looking most wretchedly,

2

she ate more, and was calmer than her sister had
expected. Had she tried to speak, or had she
been conscious of half Mrs. Jennings's well-
meant but ill-judged attentions to her, this
calmness could not have been maintained ; but
not a syllable escaped her lips, and the abstrac-
tion of her thoughts preserved her in ignorance
of everything that was passing before her.

Elinor, who did justice to Mrs. Jennings's
kindness, though its effusions were often distressing, and sometimes almost ridiculous, made
her those acknowledgments, and returned her
those civilities, which her sister could not make
or return for herself. Their good friend saw
that Marianne was unhappy, and felt that everything was due to her which might make her at
all less so. She treated her, therefore, with all
the indulgent fondness of a parent towards a
favourite child on the last day of its holidays.
Marianne was to have the best place by the fire,
was to be tempted to eat by every delicacy in
the house, and to be amused by the relation of
all the news of the day. Had not Elinor, in the
sad countenance of her sister, seen a check to all
mirth, she could have been entertained by Mrs.
Jennings's endeavours to cure a disappointment
in love, by a variety of sweetmeats and olives,
and a good fire. As soon, however, as the consciousness of all this was forced by continual

repetition on Marianne, she could stay no longer. With an hasty exclamation of misery, and a sign to her sister not to follow her, she directly got up and hurried out of the room.

'Poor soul!' cried Mrs. Jennings, as soon as she was gone, 'how it grieves me to see her! And I declare if she is not gone away without finishing her wine! And the dried cherries too! Lord! nothing seems to do her any good. I am sure if I knew of anything she would like, I would send all over the town for it. Well, it is the oddest thing to me, that a man should use such a pretty girl so ill! But when there is plenty of money on one side, and next to none on the other, Lord bless you! they care no more about such things—— !'

'The lady then—Miss Grey, I think you called her—is very rich?'

'Fifty thousand pounds, my dear. Did you ever see her? a smart, stylish girl, they say, but not handsome. I remember her aunt very well, Biddy Henshawe; she married a very wealthy man. But the family are all rich together. Fifty thousand pounds! and by all accounts it won't come before it's wanted; for they say he is all to pieces. No wonder! dashing about with his curricle and hunters! Well, it don't signify talking, but when a young man, be he who he will, comes and makes love to a pretty

4

girl, and promises marriage, he has no business to fly off from his word only because he grows poor, and a richer girl is ready to have him. Why don't he, in such a case, sell his horses, let his house, turn off his servants, and make a thorough reform at once? I warrant you, Miss Marianne would have been ready to wait till matters came round. But that won't do nowa-days; nothing in the way of pleasure can ever be given up by the young men of this age.'

'Do you know what kind of a girl Miss Grey is? Is she said to be amiable?'

'I never heard any harm of her; indeed, I hardly ever heard her mentioned; except that Mrs. Taylor did say this morning, that one day Miss Walker hinted to her, that she believed Mr. and Mrs. Ellison would not be sorry to have Miss Grey married, for she and Mrs. Ellison could never agree.'

'And who are the Ellisons?'

'Her guardians, my dear. But now she is of age and may choose for herself; and a pretty choice she has made!—What now,' after pausing a moment—'your poor sister has gone to her own room, I suppose, to moan by herself. Is there nothing one can get to comfort her? Poor dear, it seems quite cruel to let her be alone. Well, by and by we shall have a few friends, and that will amuse her a little. What shall we play at? She hates whist, I know; but is there no round game she cares for?'

'Dear ma'am, this kindness is quite unnecessary. Marianne, I dare say, will not leave her room again this evening. I shall persuade her, if I can, to go early to bed, for I am sure she wants rest.'

'Ay, I believe that will be best for her. Let her name her own supper and go to bed. Lord! no wonder she has been looking so bad and so cast-down this last week or two, for this matter, I suppose, has been hanging over her head as long as that. And so the letter that came to-day finished it! Poor soul! I am sure if I had had a notion of it I would not have joked her about it for all my money. But then, you know, how should I guess such a thing? I made sure of its being nothing but a common love-letter, and you know how young people like to be laughed at about them. Lord! how concerned Sir John and my daughters will be when they hear it! If I had had my senses about me, I might have called in Conduit Street in my way home, and told them of it. But I shall see them to-morrow.'

'It would be unnecessary, I am sure, for you to caution Mrs. Palmer and Sir John against ever naming Mr. Willoughby, or making the slightest allusion to what has passed, before my sister. Their own good-nature must point out to them the real cruelty of appearing to know anything about it when she is present; and the less that may ever be said to myself on the subject, the more my feelings will be spared, as you, my dear madam, will easily believe.'

'O Lord! yes, that I do indeed. It must be terrible for you to hear it talked of; and as for your sister, I am sure I would not mention a word about it to her for the world. You saw I did not all dinner-time. No more would Sir John nor my daughters, for they are all very thoughtful and considerate—especially if I give them a hint, as I certainly will. For my part, I think the less that is said about such things the better, the sooner 'tis blown over and forgot. And what good does talking ever do, you know?'

'In this affair it can only do harm—more so, perhaps, than in many cases of a similar kind, for it has been attended by circumstances which, for the sake of every one concerned in it, make it unfit to become the public conversation. I must do *this* justice to Mr. Willoughby—he has broken no positive engagement with my sister.'

'Law, my dear! Don't pretend to defend him. No positive engagement indeed! after taking her all over Allenham House, and fixing

7

on the very rooms they were to live in here-after!'

Elinor, for her sister's sake, could not press the subject farther, and she hoped it was not required of her for Willoughby's; since, though Marianne might lose much, he could gain very little by the enforcement of the real truth. After a short silence on both sides Mrs. Jennings, with all her natural hilarity, burst forth again—

'Well, my dear, 'tis a true saying about an ill wind, for it will be all the better for Colonel Brandon. He will have her at last; ay, that he will. Mind me, now, if they an't married by Midsummer. Lord! how he'll chuckle over this news! I hope he will come to-night. It will be all to one a better match for your sister. Two thousand a year without debt or draw-back—except the little love-child, indeed; ay, I had forgot her; but she may be 'prenticed out at small cost, and then what does it signify? Delaford is a nice place, I can tell you; exactly what I call a nice old-fashioned place, full of comforts and conveniences; quite shut in with great garden-walls that are covered with the best fruit-trees in the country; and such a mulberry tree in one corner! Lord! how Charlotte and I did stuff the only time we were there! Then, there is a dovecote, some delightful stewponds, and a very pretty canal; and everything, in short, that one could wish for: and, moreover, it is close to the church, and only a quarter of a mile from the turnpike-road, so 'tis never dull, for if you only go and sit up in an old yew arbour behind the house, you may see all the carriages that pass along. Oh! 'tis a nice place! A butcher hard by in the village, and the parsonage-house within a stone's-throw. To my fancy, a thousand times prettier than Barton Park, where they are forced to send three miles for their meat, and have not a neighbour nearer than your mother. Well, I shall spirit up the Colonel as soon as I can. One shoulder of mutton, you know, drives another down. If we *can* but put Willoughby out of her head!'

'Ay, if we can but do *that*, ma'am,' said Elinor, 'we shall do very well with or without Colonel Brandon.' And then rising, she went away to join Marianne, whom she found, as she expected, in her own room, leaning, in silent misery, over the small remains of a fire which, till Elinor's entrance, had been her only light.

'You had better leave me,' was all the notice that her sister received from her.

'I will leave you,' said Elinor, 'if you will go to bed.' But this, from the momentary perverseness of impatient suffering, she at first

refused to do. Her sister's earnest, though
gentle persuasion, however, soon softened her
to compliance, and Elinor saw her lay her
aching head on the pillow, and saw her, as she
hoped, in a way to get some quiet rest before
she left her.

In the drawing-room, whither she then re-
paired, she was soon joined by Mrs. Jennings,
with a wine-glass, full of something, in her hand.

'My dear,' said she, entering, 'I have just
recollected that I have some of the finest old
Constantia wine in the house that ever was
tasted, so I have brought a glass of it for your
sister. My poor husband! how fond he was of
it! Whenever he had a touch of his old cholicky
gout, he said it did him more good than anything else in the world. Do take it to your
sister.'

'Dear ma'am,' replied Elinor, smiling at the
difference of the complaints for which it was
recommended, 'how good you are! But I have
just left Marianne in bed, and, I hope, almost
asleep; and as I think nothing will be of so
much service to her as rest, if you would give
me leave, I will drink the wine myself.'

Mrs. Jennings, though regretting that she had
not been five minutes earlier, was satisfied with
the compromise; and Elinor, as she swallowed
the chief of it, reflected that, though its good

effects on a cholicky gout were at present of little importance to her, its healing powers on a disappointed heart might be as reasonably tried on herself as on her sister.

Colonel Brandon came in while the party were at tea, and by his manner of looking round the room for Marianne, Elinor immediately fancied that he neither expected nor wished to see her there, and, in short, that he was already aware of what occasioned her absence. Mrs. Jennings was not struck by the same thought; for, soon after his entrance, she walked across the room to the tea-table where Elinor presided, and whispered—'The Colonel looks as grave as ever, you see. He knows nothing of it; do tell him, my dear.'

He shortly afterwards drew a chair close to hers, and, with a look which perfectly assured her of his good information, inquired after her sister.

'Marianne is not well,' said she. 'She has been indisposed all day; and we have persuaded her to go to bed.'

'Perhaps, then,' he hesitatingly replied, 'what I heard this morning may be true—there may be more truth in it than I could believe possible at first.'

'What did you hear?'

''That a gentleman, whom I had reason to

11

think—in short, that a man, whom I *knew* to be engaged—but how shall I tell you? If you know it already, as surely you must, I may be spared.'

'You mean,' answered Elinor, with forced calmness, 'Mr. Willoughby's marriage with Miss Grey. Yes, we *do* know it all. This seems to have been a day of general elucidation, for this very morning first unfolded it to us. Mr. Willoughby is unfathomable! Where did you hear it?'

'In a stationer's shop in Pall Mall, where I had business. Two ladies were waiting for their carriage, and one of them was giving the other an account of the intended match, in a voice so little attempting concealment, that it was impossible for me not to hear all. The name of Willoughby, John Willoughby, frequently repeated, first caught my attention, and what followed was a positive assertion that everything was now finally settled respecting his marriage with Miss Grey—it was no longer to be a secret —it would take place even within a few weeks, with many particulars of preparation and other matters. One thing, especially, I remember, because it served to identify the man still more; —as soon as the ceremony was over they were to go to Combe Magna, his seat in Somerset-shire. My astonishment!—but it would be

12

impossible to describe what I felt. The communicative lady, I learnt on inquiry, for I staid in the shop till they were gone, was a Mrs. Ellison, and that, as I have been since informed, is the name of Miss Grey's guardian.'

'It is. But have you likewise heard that Miss Grey has fifty thousand pounds? In that, if in anything, we may find an explanation.'

'It may be so; but Willoughby is capable— at least I think'—he stopped a moment; then added in a voice which seemed to distrust itself, 'And your sister—how did she——'

'Her sufferings have been very severe. I have only to hope that they may be proportionally short. It has been, it is a most cruel affliction. Till yesterday, I believe, she never doubted his regard; and even now, perhaps— but *I* am almost convinced that he never was really attached to her. He has been very deceitful! and, in some points, there seems a hardness of heart about him.'

'Ah!' said Colonel Brandon, 'there is indeed! But your sister does not—I think you said so— she does not consider it quite as you do?'

'You know her disposition, and may believe how eagerly she would still justify him if she could.'

He made no answer; and soon afterwards, by the removal of the tea-things, and the arrange-

13

ment of the card - parties, the subject was necessarily dropped. Mrs. Jennings, who had watched them with pleasure while they were talking, and who expected to see the effect of Miss Dashwood's communication, in such an instantaneous gaiety on Colonel Brandon's side as might have become a man in the bloom of youth, of hope and happiness, saw him, with amazement, remain the whole evening more serious and thoughtful than usual.

CHAPTER XXXI

FROM a night of more sleep than she had expected, Marianne awoke the next morning to the same consciousness of misery in which she had closed her eyes.

Elinor encouraged her as much as possible to talk of what she felt; and before breakfast was ready they had gone through the subject again and again; with the same steady conviction and affectionate counsel on Elinor's side, the same impetuous feelings and varying opinions on Marianne's, as before. Sometimes she could believe Willoughby to be as unfortunate and as innocent as herself, and at others, lost every consolation in the impossibility of acquitting him. At one moment she was absolutely indifferent to the observation of all the world, at another she would seclude herself from it for ever, and at a third could resist it with energy. In one thing, however, she was uniform, when it came to the point, in avoiding, where it was possible, the presence of Mrs. Jennings, and in a determined silence when obliged to endure it. Her heart was hardened against the belief of Mrs. Jennings's entering into her sorrows with any compassion.

'No, no, no, it cannot be,' she cried; 'she cannot feel. Her kindness is not sympathy; her good-nature is not tenderness. All that she wants is gossip, and she only likes me now because I supply it.'

Elinor had not needed this to be assured of the injustice to which her sister was often led in her opinion of others, by the irritable refinement of her own mind, and the too great importance placed by her on the delicacies of a strong sensibility, and the graces of a polished manner. Like half the rest of the world, if more than half there be that are clever and good, Marianne, with excellent abilities and an excellent disposition, was neither reasonable nor candid. She expected from other people the same opinions and feelings as her own, and she judged of their motives by the immediate effect of their actions on herself. Thus a circumstance occurred, while the sisters were together in their own room after breakfast, which sunk the heart of Mrs. Jennings still lower in her estimation; because, through her own weakness, it chanced to prove a source of fresh pain to herself, though Mrs. Jennings was governed in it by an impulse of the utmost good-will.

16

SENSE AND SENSIBILITY

With a letter in her outstretched hand, and countenance gaily smiling, from the persuasion of bringing comfort, she entered their room, saying—

'Now, my dear, I bring you something that I am sure will do you good.'

Marianne heard enough. In one moment her imagination placed before her a letter from Willoughby, full of tenderness and contrition, explanatory of all that had passed, satisfactory, convincing; and instantly followed by Willoughby himself, rushing eagerly into the room to enforce, at her feet, by the eloquence of his eyes, the assurances of his letter. The work of one moment was destroyed by the next. The handwriting of her mother, never till then unwelcome, was before her; and, in the acuteness of the disappointment which followed such an ecstasy of more than hope, she felt as if, till that instant, she had never suffered.

The cruelty of Mrs. Jennings no language, within her reach in her moments of happiest eloquence, could have expressed; and now she could reproach her only by the tears which streamed from her eyes with passionate violence —a reproach, however, so entirely lost on its object, that, after many expressions of pity, she withdrew, still referring her to the letter for comfort. But the letter, when she was calm enough to read it, brought little comfort. Willoughby filled every page. Her mother, still confident of her engagement, and relying as warmly as ever on his constancy, had only been roused by Elinor's application to entreat from Marianne greater openness towards them both, and this, with such tenderness towards her, such affection for Willoughby, and such a conviction of their future happiness in each other, that she wept with agony through the whole of it.

All her impatience to be at home again now returned; her mother was dearer to her than ever — dearer through the very excess of her mistaken confidence in Willoughby, and she was wildly urgent to be gone. Elinor, unable herself to determine whether it were better for Marianne to be in London or at Barton, offered no counsel of her own except of patience till their mother's wishes could be known; and at length she obtained her sister's consent to wait for that knowledge.

Mrs. Jennings left them earlier than usual; for she could not be easy till the Middletons and Palmers were able to grieve as much as herself; and positively refusing Elinor's offered attendance, went out alone for the rest of the morning. Elinor, with a very heavy heart, aware of the pain she was going to communicate, and perceiving by Marianne's letter how ill she had succeeded in laying any foundation for it, then sat down to write her mother an account of what had passed, and entreat her directions for the future; while Marianne, who came into the drawing-room on Mrs. Jennings's going away, remained fixed at the table where Elinor wrote, watching the advancement of her pen, grieving over her for the hardship of such a task, and grieving still more fondly over its effect on her mother.

In this manner they had continued about a quarter of an hour, when Marianne, whose nerves could not then bear any sudden noise, was startled by a rap at the door.

'Who can this be?' cried Elinor. 'So early too! I thought we *had* been safe.'

Marianne moved to the window.

'It is Colonel Brandon!' said she, with vexation. 'We are never safe from *him*.'

'He will not come in, as Mrs. Jennings is from home.'

'I will not trust to *that*,' retreating to her own room. 'A man who has nothing to do with his own time has no conscience in his intrusion on that of others.'

The event proved her conjecture right, though it was founded on injustice and error, for Colonel Brandon *did* come in; and Elinor, who was convinced that solicitude for Marianne brought him thither, and who saw *that* solicitude in his disturbed and melancholy look, and in his anxious though brief inquiry after her, could not forgive her sister for esteeming him so lightly.

' I met Mrs. Jennings in Bond Street,' said he, after the first salutation, 'and she encouraged me to come on; and I was the more easily encouraged, because I thought it probable that I might find you alone, which I was very desirous of doing. My object—my wish—my sole wish in desiring it—I hope, I believe it is—is to be a means of giving comfort—no, I must not say comfort—not present comfort—but conviction, lasting conviction to your sister's mind. My regard for her, for yourself, for your mother —will you allow me to prove it by relating some circumstances, which nothing but a *very* sincere regard—nothing but an earnest desire of being useful—— I think I am justified—though where so many hours have been spent in convincing myself that I am right, is there not some reason to fear I may be wrong?' He stopped.

' I understand you,' said Elinor. ' You have something to tell me of Mr. Willoughby, that will open his character farther. Your telling it will be the greatest act of friendship that can be shewn to Marianne. *My* gratitude will be insured immediately by any information tending to that end, and *hers* must be gained by it in time. Pray, pray, let me hear it.'

'You shall; and, to be brief, when I quitted Barton last October—but this will give you no idea. I must go farther back. You will find me a very awkward narrator, Miss Dashwood; I hardly know where to begin. A short account of myself, I believe, will be necessary, and it *shall* be a short one. On such a subject,' sighing heavily, 'I can have little temptation to be diffuse.'

He stopped a moment for recollection, and then, with another sigh, went on.

'You have probably entirely forgotten a conversation—(it is not to be supposed that it could make any impression on you)—a conversation between us one evening at Barton Park—it was the evening of a dance—in which I alluded to a lady I had once known, as resembling, in some measure, your sister Marianne.'

'Indeed,' answered Elinor, 'I have *not* forgotten it.' He looked pleased by this remembrance, and added—

'If I am not deceived by the uncertainty, the partiality of tender recollection, there is a very strong resemblance between them, as well in mind as person—the same warmth of heart, the same eagerness of fancy and spirits. This lady was one of my nearest relations, an orphan from

her infancy, and under the guardianship of my
father. Our ages were nearly the same, and
from our earliest years we were playfellows and
friends. I cannot remember the time when I
did not love Eliza; and my affection for her, as
we grew up, was such, as perhaps, judging from
my present forlorn and cheerless gravity, you
might think me incapable of having ever felt.
Hers, for me, was, I believe, fervent as the
attachment of your sister to Mr. Willoughby,
and it was, though from a different cause, no
less unfortunate. At seventeen she was lost to
me for ever. She was married—married against
her inclination to my brother. Her fortune was
large, and our family estate much encumbered.
And this, I fear, is all that can be said for the
conduct of one who was at once her uncle and
guardian. My brother did not deserve her; he
did not even love her. I had hoped that her
regard for me would support her under any difficulty, and for some time it did;—but at last the
misery of her situation, for she experienced great
unkindness, overcame all her resolution, and
though she had promised me that nothing—but
how blindly I relate! I have never told you
how this was brought on. We were within a
few hours of eloping together for Scotland. The
treachery, or the folly, of my cousin's maid
betrayed us. I was banished to the house of a

relation far distant, and she was allowed no liberty, no society, no amusement, till my father's point was gained. I had depended on her fortitude too far, and the blow was a severe one—but had her marriage been happy, so young as I then was, a few months must have reconciled me to it, or at least I should not have now to lament it. This, however, was not the case. My brother had no regard for her; his pleasures were not what they ought to have been, and from the first he treated her unkindly. The consequence of this, upon a mind so young, so lively, so inexperienced as Mrs. Brandon's, was but too natural. She resigned herself at first to all the misery of her situation; and happy had it been if she had not lived to overcome those regrets which the remembrance of me occasioned. But can we wonder that with such an husband to provoke inconstancy, and without a friend to advise or restrain her (for my father lived only a few months after their marriage, and I was with my regiment in the East Indies), she should fall? Had I remained in England, perhaps—but I meant to promote the happiness of both by removing from her for years, and for that purpose had procured my exchange. The shock which her marriage had given me,' he continued in a voice of great agitation, ' was of trifling weight—was nothing—

to what I felt when I heard, about two years afterwards, of her divorce. It was *that* which threw this gloom—even now the recollection of what I suffered——'

He could say no more, and, rising hastily, walked for a few minutes about the room. Elinor, affected by his relation, and still more by his distress, could not speak. He saw her concern, and coming to her, took her hand, pressed it, and kissed it with grateful respect. A few minutes more of silent exertion enabled him to proceed with composure.

'It was nearly three years after this unhappy period before I returned to England. My first care, when I *did* arrive, was of course to seek for her; but the search was as fruitless as it was melancholy. I could not trace her beyond her first seducer, and there was every reason to fear that she had removed from him only to sink deeper in a life of sin. Her legal allowance was not adequate to her fortune, nor sufficient for her comfortable maintenance, and I learnt from my brother that the power of receiving it had been made over some months before to another person. He imagined, and calmly could he imagine it, that her extravagance and consequent distress had obliged her to dispose of it for some immediate relief. At last, however, and after I had been six months in England, I

did find her. Regard for a former servant of
my own, who had since fallen into misfortune,
carried me to visit him in a spunging-house,
where he was confined for debt; and there, in
the same house, under a similar confinement,
was my unfortunate sister. So altered—so faded
—worn down by acute suffering of every kind!
hardly could I believe the melancholy and sickly
figure before me to be the remains of the lovely,
blooming, healthful girl, on whom I had once
doated. What I endured in so beholding her—
but I have no right to wound your feelings by
attempting to describe it—I have pained you too
much already. That she was, to all appearance,
in the last stage of a consumption, was—yes,
in such a situation it was my greatest comfort.
Life could do nothing for her, beyond giving
time for a better preparation for death; and
that was given. I saw her placed in comfortable
lodgings, and under proper attendants; I visited
her every day during the rest of her short life:
I was with her in her last moments.'

Again he stopped to recover himself; and
Elinor spoke her feelings in an exclamation of
tender concern at the fate of his unfortunate
friend.

'Your sister, I hope, cannot be offended,' said
he, 'by the resemblance I have fancied between
her and my poor disgraced relation. Their fates,

their fortunes cannot be the same; and had the natural sweet disposition of the one been guarded by a firmer mind, or a happier marriage, she might have been all that you will live to see the other be. But to what does all this lead? I seem to have been distressing you for nothing. Ah! Miss Dashwood—a subject such as this—untouched for fourteen years—it is dangerous to handle it at all! I *will* be more collected—more concise. She left to my care her only little child, a little girl, the offspring of her first guilty connexion, who was then about three years old. She loved the child, and had always kept it with her. It was a valued, a precious trust to me; and gladly would I have discharged it in the strictest sense, by watching over her education myself, had the nature of our situations allowed it; but I had no family, no home; and my little Eliza was therefore placed at school. I saw her there whenever I could, and after the death of my brother (which happened about five years ago, and which left me the possession of the family property) she frequently visited me at Delaford. I called her a distant relation; but I am well aware that I have in general been suspected of a much nearer connexion with her. It is now three years ago (she had just reached her fourteenth year), that I removed her from school, to place her under the care of a very

26

respectable woman, residing in Dorsetshire, who had the charge of four or five other girls of about the same time of life ; and for two years I had every reason to be pleased with her situation. But last February, almost a twelvemonth back, she suddenly disappeared. I had allowed her (imprudently, as it has since turned out), at her earnest desire, to go to Bath with one of her young friends, who was attending her father there for his health. I knew him to be a very good sort of man, and I thought well of his daughter—better than she deserved, for, with a most obstinate and ill-judged secrecy, she would tell nothing, would give no clue, though she certainly knew all. He, her father, a well-meaning, but not a quick-sighted man, could really, I believe, give no information ; for he had been generally confined to the house, while the girls were ranging over the town and making what acquaintances they chose ; and he tried to convince me, as thoroughly as he was convinced himself, of his daughter's being entirely unconcerned in the business. In short, I could learn nothing but that she was gone ; all the rest, for eight long months, was left to conjecture. What I thought, what I feared, may be imagined ; and what I suffered too.'

'Good heavens !' cried Elinor, 'could it be ! could Willoughby——'

'The first news that reached me of her,' he continued, 'came in a letter from herself last October. It was forwarded to me from Delaford, and I received it on the very morning of our intended party to Whitwell; and this was the reason of my leaving Barton so suddenly, which I am sure must at the time have appeared strange to everybody, and which I believe gave offence to some. Little did Mr. Willoughby imagine, I suppose, when his looks censured me for incivility in breaking up the party, that I was called away to the relief of one whom he had made poor and miserable; but *had* he known it, what would it have availed? Would he have been less gay or less happy in the smiles of your sister? No, he has already done that which no man who *can* feel for another would do. He had left the girl, whose youth and innocence he had seduced, in a situation of the utmost distress, with no creditable home, no help, no friends, ignorant of his address! He had left her, promising to return; he neither returned, nor wrote, nor relieved her.'

'This is beyond everything!' exclaimed Elinor.

'His character is now before you—expensive, dissipated, and worse than both. Knowing all this, as I have now known it many weeks, guess what I must have felt on seeing your sister as

28

fond of him as ever, and on being assured that she was to marry him; guess what I must have felt for all your sakes. When I came to you last week and found you alone, I came determined to know the truth, though irresolute what to do when it *was* known. My behaviour must have seemed strange to you then; but now you will comprehend it. To suffer you all to be so deceived; to see your sister—but what could I do? I had no hope of interfering with success; and sometimes I thought your sister's influence might yet reclaim him. But now, after such dishonourable usage, who can tell what were his designs on her? Whatever they may have been, however, she may now, and hereafter doubtless *will*, turn with gratitude towards her own condition, when she compares it with that of my poor Eliza, when she considers the wretched and hopeless situation of this poor girl, and pictures her to herself, with an affection for him as strong, still as strong as her own, and with a mind tormented by self-reproach, which must attend her through life. Surely this comparison must have its use with her. She will feel her own sufferings to be nothing. They proceed from no misconduct, and can bring no disgrace. On the contrary, every friend must be made still more her friend by them. Concern for her unhappiness, and respect for her fortitude under it, must strengthen every attachment. Use your own discretion, however, in communicating to her what I have told you. You must know best what will be its effect; but had I not seriously and from my heart believed it might be of service, might lessen her regrets, I would not have suffered myself to trouble you with this account of my family afflictions, with a recital which may seem to have been intended to raise myself at the expense of others.'

Elinor's thanks followed this speech with grateful earnestness; attended, too, with the assurance of her expecting material advantage to Marianne from the communication of what had passed.

'I have been more pained,' said she, 'by her endeavours to acquit him than by all the rest; for it irritates her mind more than the most perfect conviction of his unworthiness can do. Now, though at first she will suffer much, I am sure she will soon become easier. Have you,' she continued, after a short silence, 'ever seen Mr. Willoughby since you left him at Barton?'

'Yes,' he replied gravely, 'once I have. One meeting was unavoidable.'

Elinor, startled by his manner, looked at him anxiously, saying—

'What! have you met him to——'

'I could meet him in no other way. Eliza had confessed to me, though most reluctantly, the name of her lover; and when he returned to town, which was within a fortnight after myself, we met by appointment, he to defend, I to punish his conduct. We returned unwounded, and the meeting, therefore, never got abroad.'

Elinor sighed over the fancied necessity of this; but to a man and a soldier she presumed not to censure it.

'Such,' said Colonel Brandon, after a pause, 'has been the unhappy resemblance between the fate of mother and daughter! and so imperfectly have I discharged my trust!'

'Is she still in town?'

'No; as soon as she recovered from her lying-in, for I found her near her delivery, I removed her and her child into the country, and there she remains.'

Recollecting, soon afterwards, that he was probably dividing Elinor from her sister, he put an end to his visit, receiving from her again the same grateful acknowledgments, and leaving her full of compassion and esteem for him.

CHAPTER XXXII

WHEN the particulars of this conversation were repeated by Miss Dashwood to her sister, as they very soon were, their effect on her was not entirely such as the former had hoped to see. Not that Marianne appeared to distrust the truth of any part of it, for she listened to it all with the most steady and submissive attention, made neither objection nor remark, attempted no vindication of Willoughby, and seemed to shew by her tears that she felt it to be impossible. But though this behaviour assured Elinor that the conviction of his guilt *was* carried home to her mind; though she saw with satisfaction the effect of it, in her no longer avoiding Colonel Brandon when he called, in her speaking to him, even voluntarily speaking, with a kind of compassionate respect, and though she saw her spirits less violently irritated than before; she did not see her less wretched. Her mind did become settled, but it was settled in a gloomy dejection. She felt the loss of Willoughby's character yet

more heavily than she had felt the loss of his
heart ; his seduction and desertion of Miss
Williams, the misery of that poor girl, and the
doubt of what his designs might *once* have been
on herself, preyed altogether so much on her
spirits, that she could not bring herself to speak
of what she felt even to Elinor ; and, brooding
over her sorrows in silence, gave more pain to
her sister than could have been communicated
by the most open and most frequent confession
of them.

To give the feelings or the language of Mrs.
Dashwood, on receiving and answering Elinor's
letter, would be only to give a repetition of what
her daughters had already felt and said; of a disappointment hardly less painful than Marianne's,
and an indignation even greater than Elinor's.
Long letters from her, quickly succeeding each
other, arrived to tell all that she suffered and
thought ; to express her anxious solicitude for
Marianne, and entreat she would bear up with
fortitude under this misfortune. Bad indeed
must the nature of Marianne's affliction be, when
her mother could talk of fortitude ! mortifying
and humiliating must be the origin of those
regrets which *she* could wish her not to indulge !

Against the interest of her own individual
comfort Mrs. Dashwood had determined that

it would be better for Marianne to be anywhere, at that time, than at Barton, where everything within her view would be bringing back the past in the strongest and most afflicting manner, by constantly placing Willoughby before her, such as she had always seen him there. She recommended it to her daughters, therefore, by all means not to shorten their visit to Mrs. Jennings; the length of which, though never exactly fixed, had been expected by all to comprise at least five or six weeks. A variety of occupations, of objects, and of company, which could not be procured at Barton, would be inevitable there, and might yet, she hoped, cheat Marianne, at times, into some interest beyond herself, and even into some amusement, much as the idea of both might now be spurned by her.

From all danger of seeing Willoughby again her mother considered her to be at least equally safe in town as in the country, since his acquaintance must now be dropped by all who call themselves her friends. Design could never bring them in each other's way; negligence could never leave them exposed to a surprise; and chance had less in its favour in the crowd of London than even in the retirement of Barton, where it might force him before her while paying that visit at Allenham on his marriage, which Mrs. Dashwood, from foreseeing at first as a probable event, had brought herself to expect as a certain one.

She had yet another reason for wishing her children to remain where they were: a letter from her son-in-law had told her that he and his wife were to be in town before the middle of February, and she judged it right that they should sometimes see their brother.

Marianne had promised to be guided by her mother's opinion, and she submitted to it, therefore, without opposition; though it proved perfectly different from what she wished and expected, though she felt it to be entirely wrong, formed on mistaken grounds, and that by requiring her longer continuance in London it deprived her of the only possible alleviation of her wretchedness, the personal sympathy of her mother, and doomed her to such society and such scenes as must prevent her ever knowing a moment's rest.

But it was a matter of great consolation to her, that what brought evil to herself would bring good to her sister; and Elinor, on the other hand, suspecting that it would not be in her power to avoid Edward entirely, comforted herself by thinking that, though their longer stay would therefore militate against her own happiness, it would be better for Marianne than an immediate return into Devonshire.

Her carefulness in guarding her sister from ever hearing Willoughby's name mentioned was not thrown away. Marianne, though without knowing it herself, reaped all its advantage; for neither Mrs. Jennings, nor Sir John, nor even Mrs. Palmer herself, ever spoke of him before her. Elinor wished that the same forbearance could have extended towards herself, but that was impossible, and she was obliged to listen day after day to the indignation of them all.

Sir John could not have thought it possible. 'A man of whom he had always had such reason to think well! Such a good-natured fellow! He did not believe there was a bolder rider in England! It was an unaccountable business. He wished him at the devil with all his heart. He would not speak another word to him, meet him where he might, for all the world! No, not if it were to be by the side of Barton covert, and they were kept waiting for two hours together. Such a scoundrel of a fellow! such a deceitful dog! It was only the last time they met that he had offered him one of Folly's puppies! and this was the end of it!'

Mrs. Palmer, in her way, was equally angry. 'She was determined to drop his acquaintance immediately, and she was very thankful that she had never been acquainted with him at all.

She wished with all her heart Combe Magna was not so near Cleveland; but it did not signify, for it was a great deal too far off to visit; she hated him so much that she was resolved never to mention his name again, and she should tell everybody she saw how good-for-nothing he was.'

The rest of Mrs. Palmer's sympathy was shewn in procuring all the particulars in her power of the approaching marriage, and communicating them to Elinor. She could soon tell at what coachmaker's the new carriage was building, by what painter Mr. Willoughby's portrait was drawn, and at what warehouse Miss Grey's clothes might be seen.

The calm and polite unconcern of Lady Middleton on the occasion was a happy relief to Elinor's spirits, oppressed as they often were by the clamorous kindness of the others. It was a great comfort to her to be sure of exciting no interest in *one* person at least among their circle of friends; a great comfort to know that there was *one* who would meet her without feeling any curiosity after particulars, or any anxiety for her sister's health.

Every qualification is raised at times, by the circumstances of the moment, to more than its real value; and she was sometimes worried down by officious condolence to rate good-breeding

2 c*　　　　　　　　　　　　37

as more indispensable to comfort than good-nature.

Lady Middleton expressed her sense of the affair about once every day, or twice, if the subject occurred very often, by saying, 'It is very shocking indeed!' and, by the means of this continual though gentle vent, was able not only to see the Miss Dashwoods from the first without the smallest emotion, but very soon to see them without recollecting a word of the matter; and having thus supported the dignity of her own sex, and spoken her decided censure of what was wrong in the other, she thought herself at liberty to attend to the interest of her own assemblies, and therefore determined (though rather against the opinion of Sir John), as Mrs. Willoughby would at once be a woman of elegance and fortune, to leave her card with her as soon as she married.

Colonel Brandon's delicate, unobtrusive inquiries were never unwelcome to Miss Dashwood. He had abundantly earned the privilege of intimate discussion of her sister's disappointment by the friendly zeal with which he had endeavoured to soften it, and they always conversed with confidence. His chief reward for the painful exertion of disclosing past sorrows and present humiliations was given in the pitying eye with which Marianne sometimes observed him, and the gentleness of her voice whenever (though it did not often happen) she was obliged, or could oblige herself, to speak to him. *These* assured him that his exertion had produced an increase of goodwill towards himself, and *these* gave Elinor hopes of its being farther augmented hereafter; but Mrs. Jennings, who knew nothing of all this—who knew only that the Colonel continued as grave as ever, and that she could never prevail on him to make the offer himself, nor commission her to make it for him—began at the end of two days to think that, instead of Midsummer, they would not be married till Michaelmas, and by the end of a week that it would not be a match at all. The good understanding between the Colonel and Miss Dashwood seemed rather to declare that the honours of the mulberry-tree, the canal, and the yew arbour, would all be made over to *her*; and Mrs. Jennings had for some time ceased to think at all of Mr. Ferrars.

Early in February, within a fortnight from the receipt of Willoughby's letter, Elinor had the painful office of informing her sister that he was married. She had taken care to have the intelligence conveyed to herself, as soon as it was known that the ceremony was over, as she was desirous that Marianne should not receive the first notice of it from the public papers, which she saw her eagerly examining every morning.

She received the news with resolute composure: made no observation on it, and at first shed no tears; but after a short time they would burst out, and for the rest of the day she was in a state hardly less pitiable than when she first learnt to expect the event.

The Willoughbys left town as soon as they were married; and Elinor now hoped, as there could be no danger of her seeing either of them, to prevail on her sister, who had never yet left the house since the blow first fell, to go out again by degrees as she had done before.

About this time the two Miss Steeles, lately arrived at their cousin's house in Bartlett's Buildings, Holborn, presented themselves again before their more grand relations in Conduit and Berkeley Street, and were welcomed by them all with great cordiality.

Elinor only was sorry to see them. Their presence always gave her pain, and she hardly knew how to make a very gracious return to the overpowering delight of Lucy in finding her *still* in town.

'I should have been quite disappointed if I had not found you here *still*,' said she repeatedly, with a strong emphasis on the word. 'But I always thought I *should*. I was almost sure

40

you would not leave London yet awhile;
though you *told* me, you know, at Barton, that
you should not stay above a *month*. But I
thought, at the time, that you would most likely
change your mind when it came to the point.
It would have been such a great pity to have
went away before your brother and sister came.
And now, to be sure, you will be in no *hurry*
to be gone. I am amazingly glad you did not
keep to *your word*.'

Elinor perfectly understood her, and was
forced to use all her self-command to make it
appear that she did *not*.

'Well, my dear,' said Mrs. Jennings, 'and
how did you travel ?'

'Not in the stage, I assure you,' replied Miss
Steele, with quick exultation ; 'we came post all
the way, and had a very smart beau to attend
us. Dr. Davies was coming to town, and so we
thought we 'd join him in a postchaise ; and he
behaved very genteelly, and paid ten or twelve
shillings more than we did.'

'Oh, oh !' cried Mrs. Jennings, 'very pretty,
indeed! and the doctor is a single man, I
warrant you.'

'There now,' said Miss Steele, affectedly
simpering ; 'everybody laughs at me so about
the doctor, and I cannot think why. My
cousins say they are sure I have made a con-

quest; but for my part I declare I never think about him from one hour's end to another. "Lord! here comes your beau, Nancy," my cousin said t'other day, when she saw him crossing the street to the house. "My beau, indeed!" said I, "I cannot think who you mean. The doctor is no beau of mine."'

'Ay, ay, that is very pretty talking—but it won't do—the doctor is the man, I see.'

'No, indeed!' replied her cousin, with affected earnestness, 'and I beg you will contradict it if you ever hear it talked of.'

Mrs. Jennings directly gave her the gratifying assurance that she certainly would *not*, and Miss Steele was made completely happy.

'I suppose you will go and stay with your brother and sister, Miss Dashwood, when they come to town,' said Lucy, returning, after a cessation of hostile hints, to the charge.

'No, I do not think we shall.'

'Oh yes, I dare say you will.'

Elinor would not humour her by farther opposition.

'What a charming thing it is that Mrs. Dashwood can spare you both for so long a time together!'

'Long a time, indeed!' interposed Mrs. Jennings. 'Why, their visit is but just begun!'

Lucy was silenced.

'I am sorry we cannot see your sister, Miss Dashwood,' said Miss Steele. 'I am sorry she is not well'; for Marianne had left the room on their arrival.

'You are very good. My sister will be equally sorry to miss the pleasure of seeing you; but she has been very much plagued lately with nervous headaches, which make her unfit for company or conversation.'

'Oh dear, that is a great pity! but such old friends as Lucy and me!—I think she might see *us*; and I am sure we would not speak a word.'

Elinor, with great civility, declined the proposal. 'Her sister was perhaps laid down upon the bed, or in her dressing-gown, and therefore not able to come to them.'

'Oh, if that's all,' cried Miss Steele, 'we can just as well go and see *her*.'

Elinor began to find this impertinence too much for her temper; but she was saved the trouble of checking it by Lucy's sharp reprimand, which now, as on many occasions, though it did not give much sweetness to the manners of one sister, was of advantage in governing those of the other.

CHAPTER XXXIII

AFTER some opposition Marianne yielded to her sister's entreaties, and consented to go out with her and Mrs. Jennings, one morning, for half an hour. She expressly conditioned, however, for paying no visits, and would do no more than accompany them to Gray's, in Sackville Street, where Elinor was carrying on a negotiation for the exchange of a few old-fashioned jewels of her mother.

When they stopped at the door Mrs. Jennings recollected that there was a lady at the other end of the street on whom she ought to call; and as she had no business at Gray's it was resolved that, while her young friends transacted theirs, she should pay her visit, and return for them.

On ascending the stairs the Miss Dashwoods found so many people before them in the room, that there was not a person at liberty to attend to their orders; and they were obliged to wait. All that could be done was to sit down at that end of the counter which seemed to promise the quickest succession; one gentleman only was standing there, and it is probable that Elinor was not without hope of exciting his politeness to a quicker despatch. But the correctness of his eye, and the delicacy of his taste, proved to be beyond his politeness. He was giving orders for a toothpick-case for himself, and till its size, shape, and ornaments were determined—all of which, after examining and debating for a quarter of an hour over every toothpick-case in the shop, were finally arranged by his own inventive fancy —he had no leisure to bestow any other attention on the two ladies than what was comprised in three or four very broad stares; a kind of notice which served to imprint on Elinor the remembrance of a person and face of strong, natural, sterling insignificance, though adorned in the first style of fashion.

Marianne was spared from the troublesome feelings of contempt and resentment, on this impertinent examination of their features, and on the puppyism of his manner in deciding on all the different horrors of the different toothpick-cases presented to his inspection, by remaining unconscious of it all; for she was as well able to collect her thoughts within herself, and be as ignorant of what was passing around her, in Mr. Gray's shop, as in her own bedroom.

At last the affair was decided. The ivory, the gold, and the pearls, all received their appointment, and the gentleman, having named the last day on which his existence could be continued without the possession of the toothpick-case, drew on his gloves with leisurely care, and bestowing another glance on the Miss Dashwoods, but such a one as seemed rather to demand than express admiration, walked off with an happy air of real conceit and affected indifference.

Elinor lost no time in bringing her business forward, and was on the point of concluding it, when another gentleman presented himself at her side. She turned her eyes towards his face, and found him, with some surprise, to be her brother.

Their affection and pleasure in meeting was just enough to make a very creditable appearance in Mr. Gray's shop. John Dashwood was really far from being sorry to see his sisters again; it rather gave them satisfaction; and his inquiries after their mother were respectful and attentive.

Elinor found that he and Fanny had been in town two days.

'I wished very much to call upon you yesterday,' said he, 'but it was impossible, for we were obliged to take Harry to see the wild beasts at Exeter Exchange: and we spent the rest of the day with Mrs. Ferrars. Harry was vastly pleased. *This* morning I had fully intended to call on you, if I could possibly find a spare half-hour, but one has always so much to do on first coming to town! I am come here to bespeak Fanny a seal. But to-morrow I think I shall certainly be able to call in Berkeley Street, and be introduced to your friend Mrs. Jennings. I understand she is a woman of very good fortune. And the Middletons too, you must introduce me to *them*. As my mother-in-law's relations, I shall be happy to shew them every respect. They are excellent neighbours to you in the country, I understand.'

'Excellent indeed. Their attention to our comfort, their friendliness in every particular, is more than I can express.'

'I am extremely glad to hear it, upon my word; extremely glad indeed. But so it ought to be; they are people of large fortune, they are related to you, and every civility and accommodation that can serve to make your situation pleasant might be reasonably expected. And so you are most comfortably settled in your little cottage, and want for nothing. Edward brought us a most charming account of the place; the most complete thing of its kind, he said, that ever was, and you all seemed to enjoy it beyond anything. It was a great satisfaction to us to hear it, I assure you.'

Elinor did feel a little ashamed of her brother; and was not sorry to be spared the necessity of answering him by the arrival of Mrs. Jennings's servant, who came to tell her that his mistress waited for them at the door.

Mr. Dashwood attended them downstairs, was introduced to Mrs. Jennings at the door of her carriage, and repeating his hope of being able to call on them the next day, took leave.

His visit was duly paid. He came with a pretence at an apology from their sister-in-law for not coming too; 'but she was so much engaged with her mother that, really, she had no leisure for going anywhere.' Mrs. Jennings, however, assured him directly that she should not stand upon ceremony, for they were all cousins, or something like it, and she should certainly wait on Mrs. John Dashwood very soon, and bring her sisters to see her. His manners to *them*, though calm, were perfectly kind; to Mrs. Jennings, most attentively civil; and on Colonel Brandon's coming in soon after himself, he eyed him with a curiosity which seemed to say that he only wanted to know him to be rich to be equally civil to *him*.

After staying with them half an hour he asked Elinor to walk with him to Conduit

Street, and introduce him to Sir John and Lady Middleton. The weather was remarkably fine, and she readily consented. As soon as they were out of the house his inquiries began.

'Who is Colonel Brandon? Is he a man of fortune?'

'Yes; he has a very good property in Dorsetshire.'

'I am glad of it. He seems a most gentlemanlike man, and I think, Elinor, I may congratulate you on the prospect of a very respectable establishment in life.'

'Me, brother!—what do you mean?'

'He likes you. I observed him narrowly, and am convinced of it. What is the amount of his fortune?'

'I believe about two thousand a year.'

'Two thousand a year'; and then working himself up to a pitch of enthusiastic generosity, he added—

'Elinor, I wish with all my heart it were *twice* as much, for your sake.'

'Indeed I believe you,' replied Elinor, 'but I am very sure that Colonel Brandon has not the smallest wish of marrying *me*.'

'You are mistaken, Elinor; you are very much mistaken. A very little trouble on your side secures him. Perhaps just at present he may be undecided; the smallness of your fortune may make him hang back; his friends

may all advise him against it. But some of
those little attentions and encouragements which
ladies can so easily give will fix him, in spite of
himself. And there can be no reason why you
should not try for him. It is not to be supposed
that any prior attachment on your side—in
short you know, as to an attachment of that
kind, it is quite out of the question, the
objections are insurmountable—you have too
much sense not to see all that. Colonel
Brandon must be the man ; and no civility shall
be wanting on my part to make him pleased
with you and your family. It is a match that
must give universal satisfaction. In short, it is a
kind of thing that'—lowering his voice to an important whisper—' will be exceedingly welcome
to *all* parties.' Recollecting himself, however, he
added, ' That is, I mean to say—your friends are
all truly anxious to see you well settled, Fanny
particularly, for she has your interest very much
at heart, I assure you. And her mother too,
Mrs. Ferrars, a very good-natured woman, I am
sure it would give her great pleasure ; she said
as much the other day.'

Elinor would not vouchsafe any answer.

' It would be something remarkable, now,' he
continued, 'something droll, if Fanny should
have a brother and I a sister settling at the
same time. And yet it is not very unlikely.'

'Is Mr. Edward Ferrars,' said Elinor with resolution, 'going to be married?'

'It is not actually settled, but there is such a thing in agitation. He has a most excellent mother. Mrs. Ferrars, with the utmost liberality, will come forward, and settle on him a thousand a year, if the match takes place. The lady is the Honourable Miss Morton, only daughter of the late Lord Morton, with thirty thousand pounds—a very desirable connexion on both sides, and I have not a doubt of its taking place in time. A thousand a year is a great deal for a mother to give away, to make over for ever; but Mrs. Ferrars has a noble spirit. To give you another instance of her liberality:—The other day, as soon as we came to town, aware that money could not be very plenty with us just now, she put banknotes into Fanny's hands to the amount of two hundred pounds. And extremely acceptable it is, for we must live at a great expense while we are here.'

He paused for her assent and compassion; and she forced herself to say—

'Your expenses both in town and country must certainly be considerable, but your income is a large one.'

'Not so large, I dare say, as many people suppose. I do not mean to complain, however; it is undoubtedly a comfortable one, and, I hope,

will in time be better. The enclosure of Norland Common, now carrying on, is a most serious
drain. And then I have made a little purchase
within this half-year—East Kingham Farm, you
must remember the place, where old Gibson
used to live. The land was so very desirable
for me in every respect, so immediately adjoining my own property, that I felt it my duty to
buy it. I could not have answered it to my
conscience to let it fall into any other hands.
A man must pay for his convenience, and it *has*
cost me a vast deal of money.'

'More than you think it really and intrinsically
worth?'

'Why, I hope not that. I might have sold it
again, the next day, for more than I gave: but,
with regard to the purchase-money, I might
have been very unfortunate indeed; for the
stocks were at that time so low, that if I had
not happened to have the necessary sum in my
banker's hands, I must have sold out to very
great loss.'

Elinor could only smile.

'Other great and inevitable expenses, too,
we have had on first coming to Norland. Our
respected father, as you well know, bequeathed
all the Stanhill effects that remained at Norland
(and very valuable they were) to your mother.
Far be it for me to repine at his doing so; he

had an undoubted right to dispose of his own property as he chose. But in consequence of it we have been obliged to make large purchases of linen, china, etc., to supply the place of what was taken away. You may guess, after all these expenses, how very far we must be from being rich, and how acceptable Mrs. Ferrars's kindness is.'

'Certainly,' said Elinor; 'and assisted by her liberality I hope you may yet live to be in easy circumstances.'

'Another year or two may do much towards it,' he gravely replied; 'but, however, there is still a great deal to be done. There is not a stone laid of Fanny's greenhouse, and nothing but the plan of the flower-garden marked out.'

'Where is the greenhouse to be?'

'Upon the knoll behind the house. The old walnut-trees are all come down to make room for it. It will be a very fine object from many parts of the park, and the flower-garden will slope down just before it, and be exceedingly pretty. We have cleared away all the old thorns that grew in patches over the brow.'

Elinor kept her concern and her censure to herself, and was very thankful that Marianne was not present to share the provocation.

Having now said enough to make his poverty clear, and to do away the necessity of buying

2 D*   53

a pair of ear-rings for each of his sisters, in his next visit at Gray's, his thoughts took a cheerfuller turn, and he began to congratulate Elinor on having such a friend as Mrs. Jennings.

'She seems a most valuable woman indeed. Her house, her style of living, all bespeak an exceeding good income, and it is an acquaintance that has not only been of great use to you hitherto, but in the end may prove materially advantageous. Her inviting you to town is certainly a vast thing in your favour; and, indeed, it speaks altogether so great a regard for you, that in all probability when she dies you will not be forgotten. She must have a great deal to leave.'

'Nothing at all, I should rather suppose; for she has only her jointure, which will descend to her children.'

'But it is not to be imagined that she lives up to her income. Few people of common prudence will do *that*; and whatever she saves she will be able to dispose of.'

'And do you not think it more likely that she should leave it to her daughters than to us?'

'Her daughters are both exceedingly well married, and therefore I cannot perceive the necessity of her remembering them farther. Whereas, in my opinion, by her taking so much notice of you, and treating you in this kind of way, she has given you a sort of claim on her future consideration, which a conscientious woman would not disregard. Nothing can be kinder than her behaviour; and she can hardly do all this without being aware of the expectations she raises.'

'But she raises none in those most concerned. Indeed, brother, your anxiety for our welfare and prosperity carries you too far.'

'Why, to be sure,' said he, seeming to recollect himself, 'people have little, have very little, in their power. But, my dear Elinor, what is the matter with Marianne?—she looks very unwell, has lost her colour, and is grown quite thin. Is she ill?'

'She is not well; she has had a nervous complaint on her for several weeks.'

'I am sorry for that. At her time of life anything of an illness destroys the bloom for ever! Hers has been a very short one! She was as handsome a girl last September as any I ever saw, and as likely to attract the men. There was something in her style of beauty to please them particularly. I remember Fanny used to say that she would marry sooner and better than you did; not but what she is exceedingly fond of *you*—but so it happened to strike her. She will be mistaken, however. I question whether Marianne, *now*, will marry a man worth more than five or six hundred a year at the utmost, and I am very much deceived if *you* do not do better. Dorsetshire! I know very little of Dorsetshire, but, my dear Elinor, I shall be exceedingly glad to know more of it; and I think I can answer for your having Fanny and myself among the earliest and best pleased of your visitors.'

Elinor tried very seriously to convince him that there was no likelihood of her marrying Colonel Brandon; but it was an expectation of too much pleasure to himself to be relinquished, and he was really resolved on seeking an intimacy with that gentleman, and promoting the marriage by every possible attention. He had just compunction enough for having done nothing for his sisters himself, to be exceedingly anxious that everybody else should do a great deal; and an offer from Colonel Brandon, or a legacy from Mrs. Jennings, was the easiest means of atoning for his own neglect.

They were lucky enough to find Lady Middleton at home, and Sir John came in before their visit ended. Abundance of civilities passed on all sides. Sir John was ready to like anybody, and though Mr. Dashwood did not seem to know much about horses, he soon set him down as a very good-natured fellow; while Lady Middleton saw enough of fashion in his

appearance to think his acquaintance worth
having; and Mr. Dashwood went away delighted with both.

'I shall have a charming account to carry to
Fanny,' said he, as he walked back with his
sister. 'Lady Middleton is really a most elegant
woman! such a woman as, I am sure, Fanny
will be glad to know. And Mrs. Jennings
too, an exceeding well-behaved woman, though
not so elegant as her daughter. Your sister
need not have any scruple even of visiting *her*,
which, to say the truth, has been a little the
case, and very naturally; for we only knew
that Mrs. Jennings was the widow of a man
who had got all his money in a low way; and
Fanny and Mrs. Ferrars were both strongly
prepossessed that she nor her daughters were
such kind of women as Fanny would like to
associate with. But now I can carry her a most
satisfactory account of both.'

SENSE AND SENSIBILITY

CHAPTER XXXIV

MRS. JOHN DASHWOOD had so much confidence in her husband's judgment that she waited the very next day both on Mrs. Jennings and her daughter; and her confidence was rewarded by finding even the former, even the woman with whom her sisters were staying, by no means unworthy her notice; and as for Lady Middleton, she found her one of the most charming women in the world!

Lady Middleton was equally pleased with Mrs. Dashwood. There was a kind of cold-hearted selfishness on both sides, which mutually attracted them; and they sympathised with each other in an insipid propriety of demeanour and a general want of understanding.

The same manners, however, which recommended Mrs. John Dashwood to the good opinion of Lady Middleton, did not suit the fancy of Mrs. Jennings, and to *her* she appeared nothing more than a little proud-looking woman of uncordial address, who met her husband's

58

sisters without any affection, and almost without having anything to say to them; for of the quarter of an hour bestowed on Berkeley Street she sat at least seven minutes and a half in silence.

Elinor wanted very much to know, though she did not chuse to ask, whether Edward was then in town; but nothing would have induced Fanny voluntarily to mention his name before her, till able to tell her that his marriage with Miss Morton was resolved on, or till her husband's expectations on Colonel Brandon were answered; because she believed them still so very much attached to each other that they could not be too sedulously divided in word and deed on every occasion. The intelligence, however, which *she* would not give, soon flowed from another quarter. Lucy came very shortly to claim Elinor's compassion on being unable to see Edward, though he had arrived in town with Mr. and Mrs. Dashwood. He dared not come to Bartlett's Buildings for fear of detection, and though their mutual impatience to meet was not to be told, they could do nothing at present but write.

Edward assured them himself of his being in town, within a very short time, by twice calling in Berkeley Street. Twice was his card found on the table, when they returned from their

morning's engagements. Elinor was pleased
that he had called, and still more pleased that
she had missed him.

The Dashwoods were so prodigiously delighted with the Middletons that, though not
much in the habit of giving anything, they
determined to give them a dinner; and soon
after their acquaintance began, invited them to
dine in Harley Street, where they had taken
a very good house for three months. Their
sisters and Mrs. Jennings were invited likewise,
and John Dashwood was careful to secure
Colonel Brandon, who, always glad to be where
the Miss Dashwoods were, received his eager
civilities with some surprise, but much more
pleasure. They were to meet Mrs. Ferrars;
but Elinor could not learn whether her sons
were to be of the party. The expectation of
seeing *her*, however, was enough to make her
interested in the engagement; for though she
could now meet Edward's mother without that
strong anxiety which had once promised to
attend such an introduction, though she could
now see her with perfect indifference as to her
opinion of herself, her desire of being in company
with Mrs. Ferrars, her curiosity to know what
she was like, was as lively as ever.

The interest with which she thus anticipated
the party was soon afterwards increased, more

powerfully than pleasantly, by her hearing that the Miss Steeles were also to be at it.

So well had they recommended themselves to Lady Middleton, so agreeable had their assiduities made them to her, that though Lucy was certainly not elegant, and her sister not even genteel, she was as ready as Sir John to ask them to spend a week or two in Conduit Street; and it happened to be particularly convenient to the Miss Steeles, as soon as the Dashwoods' invitation was known, that their visit should begin a few days before the party took place.

Their claims to the notice of Mrs. John Dashwood, as the nieces of the gentleman who for many years had had the care of her brother, might not have done much, however, towards procuring them seats at her table; but as Lady Middleton's guests they must be welcome; and Lucy, who had long wanted to be personally known to the family, to have a nearer view of their characters and her own difficulties, and to have an opportunity of endeavouring to please them, had seldom been happier in her life than she was on receiving Mrs. John Dashwood's card.

On Elinor its effect was very different. She began immediately to determine that Edward, who lived with his mother, must be asked, as his mother was, to a party given by his sister;

and to see him for the first time, after all that passed, in the company of Lucy!—she hardly knew how she could bear it!

These apprehensions, perhaps, were not founded entirely on reason, and certainly not at all on truth. They were relieved, however, not by her own recollection, but by the goodwill of Lucy, who believed herself to be inflicting a severe disappointment when she told her that Edward certainly would not be in Harley Street on Tuesday, and even hoped to be carrying the pain still farther by persuading her, that he was kept away by that extreme affection for herself, which he could not conceal when they were together.

The important Tuesday came that was to introduce the two young ladies to this formidable mother-in-law.

'Pity me, dear Miss Dashwood!' said Lucy, as they walked up the stairs together—for the Middletons arrived so directly after Mrs. Jennings that they all followed the servant at the same time—'There is nobody here but you that can feel for me. I declare I can hardly stand. Good gracious!—in a moment I shall see the person that all my happiness depends on—that is to be my mother!'

Elinor could have given her immediate relief by suggesting the possibility of its being Miss

Morton's mother, rather than her own, whom they were about to behold ; but instead of doing that, she assured her, and with great sincerity, that she did pity her—to the utter amazement of Lucy, who, though really uncomfortable herself, hoped at least to be an object of irrepressible envy to Elinor.

Mrs. Ferrars was a little, thin woman, upright, even to formality, in her figure, and serious, even to sourness, in her aspect. Her complexion was sallow, and her features small, without beauty, and naturally without expression ; but a lucky contraction of the brow had rescued her countenance from the disgrace of insipidity by giving it the strong characters of pride and ill-nature. She was not a woman of many words ; for, unlike people in general, she proportioned them to the number of her ideas : and of the few syllables that did escape her, not one fell to the share of Miss Dashwood, whom she eyed with the spirited determination of disliking her at all events.

Elinor could not *now* be made unhappy by this behaviour. A few months ago it would have hurt her exceedingly ; but it was not in Mrs. Ferrars's power to distress her by it now ; and the difference of her manners to the Miss Steeles—a difference which seemed purposely made to humble her more—only amused her.

She could not but smile to see the graciousness of both mother and daughter towards the very person—for Lucy was particularly distinguished—whom of all others, had they known as much as she did, they would have been most anxious to mortify; while she herself, who had comparatively no power to wound them, sat pointedly slighted by both. But while she smiled at a graciousness so misapplied, she could not reflect on the mean-spirited folly from which it sprung, nor observe the studied attentions with which the Miss Steeles courted its continuance, without thoroughly despising them all four.

Lucy was all exultation on being so honourably distinguished; and Miss Steele wanted only to be teased about Dr. Davies to be perfectly happy.

The dinner was a grand one, the servants were numerous, and everything bespoke the mistress's inclination for show, and the master's ability to support it. In spite of the improvements and additions which were making to the Norland estate, and in spite of its owner having once been within some thousand pounds of being obliged to sell out at a loss, nothing gave any symptom of that indigence which he had tried to infer from it; no poverty of any kind, except of conversation, appeared—but there the deficiency was considerable. John Dashwood had not much to say for himself that was worth hearing, and his wife had still less. But there was no peculiar disgrace in this, for it was very much the case with the chief of their visitors, who almost all laboured under one or other of these disqualifications for being agreeable—want of sense, either natural or improved, want of elegance, want of spirits, or want of temper.

When the ladies withdrew to the drawing-room after dinner, this poverty was particularly evident, for the gentlemen *had* supplied the discourse with some variety — the variety of politics, enclosing land, and breaking horses— but then it was all over, and one subject only engaged the ladies till coffee came in, which was the comparative heights of Harry Dashwood and Lady Middleton's second son, William, who were nearly of the same age.

Had both the children been there, the affair might have been determined too easily by measuring them at once; but as Harry only was present, it was all conjectural assertion on both sides, and everybody had a right to be equally positive in their opinion, and to repeat it over and over again as often as they liked.

The parties stood thus—

The two mothers, though each really convinced that her own son was the tallest, politely decided in favour of the other.

The two grandmothers, with not less partiality, but more sincerity, were equally earnest in support of their own descendant.

Lucy, who was hardly less anxious to please one parent than the other, thought the boys were both remarkably tall for their age, and could not conceive that there could be the smallest difference in the world between them; and Miss Steele, with yet greater address, gave it, as fast as she could, in favour of each.

Elinor, having once delivered her opinion on William's side, by which she offended Mrs. Ferrars, and Fanny still more, did not see the necessity of enforcing it by any farther assertion; and Marianne, when called on for hers, offended them all by declaring that she had no opinion to give, as she had never thought about it.

Before her removing from Norland Elinor had painted a very pretty pair of screens for her sister-in-law, which being now just mounted and brought home, ornamented her present drawing-room; and these screens, catching the eye of John Dashwood on his following the other gentlemen into the room, were officiously handed by him to Colonel Brandon for his admiration.

'These are done by my eldest sister,' said he; 'and you, as a man of taste, will, I dare say, be pleased with them. I do not know whether you ever happened to see any of her performances before, but she is in general reckoned to draw extremely well.'

The Colonel, though disclaiming all pretensions to connoisseurship, warmly admired the screens, as he would have done anything painted by Miss Dashwood ; and the curiosity of the others being of course excited, they were handed round for general inspection. Mrs. Ferrars, not aware of their being Elinor's work, particularly requested to look at them ; and after they had received the gratifying testimony of Lady Middleton's approbation, Fanny presented them to her mother, considerately informing her at the same time that they were done by Miss Dashwood.

'Hum'—said Mrs. Ferrars—'very pretty'— and, without regarding them at all, returned them to her daughter.

Perhaps Fanny thought for a moment that her mother had been quite rude enough ; for, colouring a little, she immediately said—

'They are very pretty, ma'am—an't they?' But then again, the dread of having been too civil, too encouraging herself, probably came over her, for she presently added—

'Do you not think they are something in Miss Morton's style of painting, ma'am? *She does* paint most delightfully. How beautifully her last landscape is done!'

'Beautifully indeed. But *she* does everything well.'

Marianne could not bear this. She was already greatly displeased with Mrs. Ferrars; and such ill-timed praise of another, at Elinor's expense, though she had not any notion of what was principally meant by it, provoked her immediately to say with warmth—

'This is admiration of a very particular kind! What is Miss Morton to us? Who knows or who cares for her? It is Elinor of whom *we* think and speak.'

And so saying, she took the screens out of her sister-in-law's hands to admire them herself as they ought to be admired.

Mrs. Ferrars looked exceedingly angry, and drawing herself up more stiffly than ever, pronounced, in retort, this bitter philippic: 'Miss Morton is Lord Morton's daughter.'

Fanny looked very angry too, and her husband was all in a fright at his sister's audacity. Elinor was much more hurt by Marianne's warmth than she had been by what produced it; but Colonel Brandon's eyes, as they were fixed on Marianne, declared that he noticed only what was amiable in it: the affectionate heart which could not bear to see a sister slighted on the smallest point.

Marianne's feelings did not stop here. The

cold insolence of Mrs. Ferrars's general behaviour to her sister seemed, to her, to foretell such difficulties and distresses to Elinor as her own wounded heart taught her to think of with horror; and, urged by a strong impulse of affectionate sensibility, she moved, after a moment, to her sister's chair, and putting one arm round her neck, and one cheek close to hers, said in a low, but eager voice—

'Dear, dear Elinor, don't mind them. Don't let them make *you* unhappy.'

She could say no more: her spirits were quite overcome; and hiding her face on Elinor's shoulder, she burst into tears. Everybody's attention was called, and almost everybody was concerned. Colonel Brandon rose up and went to them without knowing what he did. Mrs. Jennings, with a very intelligent 'Ah! poor dear,' immediately gave her her salts; and Sir John felt so desperately enraged against the author of this nervous distress, that he instantly changed his seat to one close by Lucy Steele, and gave her, in a whisper, a brief account of the whole shocking affair.

In a few minutes, however, Marianne was recovered enough to put an end to the bustle, and sit down among the rest; though her spirits retained the impression of what had passed the whole evening.

2 E*

'Poor Marianne!' said her brother to Colonel Brandon in a low voice, as soon as he could secure his attention; 'she has not such good health as her sister—she is very nervous—she has not Elinor's constitution; and one must allow that there is something very trying to a young woman who *has been* a beauty, in the loss of her personal attractions. You would not think it, perhaps, but Marianne *was* remarkably handsome a few months ago—quite as handsome as Elinor. Now you see it is all gone.'

CHAPTER XXXV

ELINOR'S curiosity to see Mrs. Ferrars was satisfied. She had found in her everything that could tend to make a farther connexion between the families undesirable. She had seen enough of her pride, her meanness, and her determined prejudice against herself, to comprehend all the difficulties that must have perplexed the engagement, and retarded the marriage of Edward and herself, had he been otherwise free; and she had seen almost enough to be thankful, for her *own* sake, that one greater obstacle preserved her from suffering under any other of Mrs. Ferrars's creation, preserved her from all dependence upon her caprice, or any solicitude for her good opinion. Or at least, if she did not bring herself quite to rejoice in Edward's being fettered to Lucy, she determined that, had Lucy been more amiable, she *ought* to have rejoiced.

She wondered that Lucy's spirits could be so very much elevated by the civility of Mrs. Ferrars; that her interest and her vanity should so very much blind her as to make the attention, which seemed only paid her because she was *not Elinor*, appear a compliment to herself—or to allow her to derive encouragement from a preference only given her because her real situation was unknown. But that it was so, had not only been declared by Lucy's eyes at the time, but was declared over again the next morning more openly; for, at her particular desire, Lady Middleton set her down in Berkeley Street on the chance of seeing Elinor alone, to tell her how happy she was.

The chance proved a lucky one, for a message from Mrs. Palmer, soon after she arrived, carried Mrs. Jennings away.

'My dear friend,' cried Lucy, as soon as they were by themselves, 'I come to talk to you of my happiness. Could anything be so flattering as Mrs. Ferrars's way of treating me yesterday? So exceedingly affable as she was! You know how I dreaded the thoughts of seeing her; but the very moment I was introduced, there was such an affability in her behaviour as really should seem to say, she had quite took a fancy to me. Now was not it so? You saw it all; and was not you quite struck with it?'

'She was certainly very civil to you.'

'Civil!—Did you see nothing but only civility? I saw a vast deal more—such kindness as fell to the share of nobody but me! No pride, no hauteur, and your sister just the same—all sweetness and affability!'

Elinor wished to talk of something else, but Lucy still pressed her to own that she had reason for her happiness, and Elinor was obliged to go on.

'Undoubtedly, if they had known your engagement,' said she, 'nothing could be more flattering than their treatment of you; but as that was not the case——'

'I guessed you would say so,' replied Lucy quickly; 'but there was no reason in the world why Mrs. Ferrars should seem to like me if she did not—and her liking me is everything. You shan't talk me out of my satisfaction. I am sure it will all end well, and there will be no difficulties at all, to what I used to think. Mrs. Ferrars is a charming woman, and so is your sister. They are both delightful women indeed! —I wonder I should never hear you say how agreeable Mrs. Dashwood was?'

To this Elinor had no answer to make, and did not attempt any.

'Are you ill, Miss Dashwood?—you seem low —you don't speak;—sure, you an't well.'

'I never was in better health.'

'I am glad of it with all my heart, but really you did not look it. I should be so sorry to have *you* ill,—you, that have been the greatest comfort to me in the world!—Heaven knows what I should have done without your friendship.'

Elinor tried to make a civil answer, though doubting her own success. But it seemed to satisfy Lucy, for she directly replied—

'Indeed I am perfectly convinced of your regard for me, and next to Edward's love it is the greatest comfort I have. Poor Edward! But now, there is one good thing—we shall be able to meet, and meet pretty often, for Lady Middleton's delighted with Mrs. Dashwood, so we shall be a good deal in Harley Street, I dare say, and Edward spends half his time with his sister—besides, Lady Middleton and Mrs. Ferrars will visit now; and Mrs. Ferrars and your sister were both so good to say more than once, they should always be glad to see me.— They are such charming women!—I am sure, if ever you tell your sister what I think of her, you cannot speak too high.'

But Elinor would not give her any encouragement to hope that she *should* tell her sister. Lucy continued—

'I am sure I should have seen it in a moment if Mrs. Ferrars had took a dislike to me. If she had only made me a formal curtsey, for instance, without saying a word, and never after had took any notice of me, and never looked at me in a

pleasant way—you know what I mean—if I
had been treated in that forbidding sort of way,
I should have gave it all up in despair. I could
not have stood it. For where she *does* dislike,
I know it is most violent.'

Elinor was prevented from making any reply
to this civil triumph by the door's being thrown
open, the servant's announcing Mr. Ferrars, and
Edward's immediately walking in.

It was a very awkward moment; and the
countenance of each shewed that it was so.
They all looked exceedingly foolish; and Edward
seemed to have as great an inclination to walk
out of the room again as to advance farther into
it. The very circumstance, in its unpleasantest
form, which they would each have been most
anxious to avoid, had fallen on them—they were
not only all three together, but were together
without the relief of any other person. The
ladies recovered themselves first. It was not
Lucy's business to put herself forward, and the
appearance of secrecy must still be kept up.
She could therefore only *look* her tenderness,
and after slightly addressing him, said no more.

But Elinor had more to do; and so anxious
was she, for his sake and her own, to do it well,
that she forced herself, after a moment's recollection, to welcome him, with a look and manner
that were almost easy and almost open; and

another struggle, another effort, still improved
them. She would not allow the presence of
Lucy, nor the consciousness of some injustice
towards herself, to deter her from saying that
she was happy to see him, and that she had very
much regretted being from home when he called
before in Berkeley Street. She would not be
frightened from paying him those attentions
which, as a friend and almost a relation, were
his due, by the observant eyes of Lucy, though
she soon perceived them to be narrowly watching her.

Her manners gave some reassurance to
Edward, and he had courage enough to sit
down; but his embarrassment still exceeded
that of the ladies in a proportion which the case
rendered reasonable, though his sex might make
it rare; for his heart had not the indifference of
Lucy's, nor could his conscience have quite the
ease of Elinor's.

Lucy, with a demure and settled air, seemed
determined to make no contribution to the
comfort of the others, and would not say a
word; and almost everything that *was* said
proceeded from Elinor, who was obliged to
volunteer all the information about her mother's
health, their coming to town, etc., which
Edward ought to have inquired about, but
never did.

Her exertions did not stop here; for she soon afterwards felt herself so heroically disposed as to determine, under pretence of fetching Marianne, to leave the others by themselves; and she really did it, and *that* in the handsomest manner, for she loitered away several minutes on the landing-place, with the most high-minded fortitude, before she went to her sister. When that was once done, however, it was time for the raptures of Edward to cease; for Marianne's joy hurried her into the drawing-room immediately. Her pleasure in seeing him was like every other of her feelings, strong in itself and strongly spoken. She met him with a hand that would be taken, and a voice that expressed the affection of a sister.

' Dear Edward!' she cried, ' this is a moment of great happiness!—This would almost make amends for everything!'

Edward tried to return her kindness as it deserved, but before such witnesses he dared not say half what he really felt. Again they all sat down, and for a moment or two all were silent; while Marianne was looking with the most speaking tenderness, sometimes at Edward and sometimes at Elinor, regretting only that their delight in each other should be checked by Lucy's unwelcome presence. Edward was the first to speak, and it was to notice Marianne's

77

altered looks, and express his fear of her not finding London agree with her.

'Oh! don't think of me!' she replied, with spirited earnestness, though her eyes were filled with tears as she spoke, 'don't think of *my* health. Elinor is well, you see. That must be enough for us both.'

This remark was not calculated to make Edward or Elinor more easy, nor to conciliate the goodwill of Lucy, who looked up at Marianne with no very benignant expression.

'Do you like London?' said Edward, willing to say anything that might introduce another subject.

'Not at all. I expected much pleasure in it, but I have found none. The sight of you, Edward, is the only comfort it has afforded; and, thank Heaven! you are what you always were!'

She paused—no one spoke.

'I think, Elinor,' she presently added, 'we must employ Edward to take care of us in our return to Barton. In a week or two, I suppose, we shall be going; and, I trust, Edward will not be very unwilling to accept the charge.'

Poor Edward muttered something; but what it was nobody knew, not even himself. But Marianne, who saw his agitation, and could easily trace it to whatever cause best pleased

herself, was perfectly satisfied, and soon talked
of something else.

'We spent such a day, Edward, in Harley
Street, yesterday! So dull, so wretchedly dull!
But I have much to say to you on that head,
which cannot be said now.'

And with this admirable discretion did she
defer the assurance of her finding their mutual
relatives more disagreeable than ever, and of her
being particularly disgusted with his mother, till
they were more in private.

'But why were you not there, Edward?
Why did you not come?'

'I was engaged elsewhere.'

'Engaged! But what was that, when such
friends were to be met?'

'Perhaps, Miss Marianne,' cried Lucy, eager
to take some revenge on her, 'you think young
men never stand upon engagements, if they
have no mind to keep them, little as well as
great.'

Elinor was very angry, but Marianne seemed
entirely insensible of the sting; for she calmly
replied—

'Not so, indeed; for, seriously speaking, I am
very sure that conscience only kept Edward
from Harley Street. And I really believe he
has the most delicate conscience in the world;
the most scrupulous in performing every engage-

ment, however minute, and however it may make against his interest or pleasure. He is the most fearful of giving pain, of wounding expectation, and the most incapable of being selfish, of anybody I ever saw. Edward, it is so, and I will say it. What! are you never to hear yourself praised? Then you must be no friend of mine; for those who will accept of my love and esteem must submit to my open commendation.'

The nature of her commendation in the present case, however, happened to be particularly ill-suited to the feelings of two-thirds of her auditors, and was so very unexhilarating to Edward, that he very soon got up to go away.

'Going so soon!' said Marianne; 'my dear Edward, this must not be.'

And drawing him a little aside, she whispered her persuasion that Lucy could not stay much longer. But even this encouragement failed, for he would go; and Lucy, who would have outstaid him had his visit lasted two hours, soon afterwards went away.

'What can bring her here so often!' said Marianne, on her leaving them. 'Could she not see that we wanted her gone? How teasing to Edward!'

'Why so?—we were all his friends, and Lucy has been the longest known to him of any. It is but natural that he should like to see her as well as ourselves.'

Marianne looked at her steadily and said, 'You know, Elinor, that this is a kind of talking which I cannot bear. If you only hope to have your assertion contradicted, as I must suppose to be the case, you ought to recollect that I am the last person in the world to do it. I cannot descend to be tricked out of assurances that are not really wanted.'

She then left the room ; and Elinor dared not follow her to say more, for, bound as she was by her promise of secrecy to Lucy, she could give no information that would convince Marianne ; and painful as the consequences of her still continuing in an error might be, she was obliged to submit to it. All that she could hope, was that Edward would not often expose her or himself to the distress of hearing Marianne's mistaken warmth, nor to the repetition of any other part of the pain that had attended their recent meeting—and this she had every reason to expect.

amply rewarded for the sacrifice of the best place by the fire after dinner, which their arrival occasioned. But this conciliation was not granted; for though she often threw out expressions of pity for her sister to Elinor, and more than once dropped a reflection on the inconstancy of beaux before Marianne, no effect was produced, but a look of indifference from the former or of disgust in the latter. An effort even yet lighter might have made her their friend. Would they only have laughed at her about the doctor! But so little were they, any more than the others, inclined to oblige her, that if Sir John dined from home, she might spend a whole day without hearing any other raillery on the subject than what she was kind enough to bestow on herself.

All these jealousies and discontents, however, were so totally unsuspected by Mrs. Jennings, that she thought it a delightful thing for the girls to be together; and generally congratulated her young friends every night on having escaped the company of a stupid old woman so long. She joined them sometimes at Sir John's, and sometimes at her own house; but wherever it was, she always came in excellent spirits, full of delight and importance, attributing Charlotte's well-doing to her own care, and ready to give so exact, so minute a detail of her situa-

tion, as only Miss Steele had curiosity enough
to desire. One thing *did* disturb her; and of
that she made her daily complaint. Mr. Palmer
maintained the common, but unfatherly opinion
among his sex, of all infants being alike; and,
though she could plainly perceive at different
times the most striking resemblance between
this baby and every one of his relations on both
sides, there was no convincing his father of it;
no persuading him to believe that it was not
exactly like every other baby of the same age;
nor could he even be brought to acknowledge
the simple proposition of its being the finest
child in the world.

I come now to the relation of a misfortune
which about this time befell Mrs. John Dashwood. It so happened that while her two sisters
with Mrs. Jennings were first calling on her in
Harley Street, another of her acquaintance had
dropped in—a circumstance in itself not apparently likely to produce evil to her. But while
the imaginations of other people will carry them
away to form wrong judgments of our conduct,
and to decide on it by slight appearances, one's
happiness must in some measure be always at
the mercy of chance. In the present instance,
this last-arrived lady allowed her fancy so far to
outrun truth and probability, that on merely
hearing the name of the Miss Dashwoods, and

understanding them to be Mr. Dashwood's sisters, she immediately concluded them to be staying in Harley Street ; and this misconstruction produced within a day or two afterwards cards of invitation for them, as well as for their brother and sister, to a small musical party at her house. The consequence of which was, that Mrs. John Dashwood was obliged to submit not only to the exceedingly great inconvenience of sending her carriage for the Miss Dashwoods, but, what was still worse, must be subject to all the unpleasantness of appearing to treat them with attention : and who could tell that they might not expect to go out with her a second time ? The power of disappointing them, it was true, must always be hers. But that was not enough ; for when people are determined on a mode of conduct which they know to be wrong, they feel injured by the expectation of anything better from them.

Marianne had now been brought by degrees so much into the habit of going out every day, that it was become a matter of indifference to her whether she went or not : and she prepared quietly and mechanically for every evening's engagement, though without expecting the smallest amusement from any, and very often without knowing till the last moment where it was to take her.

To her dress and appearance she was growing so perfectly indifferent as not to bestow half the consideration on it, during the whole of her toilette, which it received from Miss Steele in the first five minutes of their being together, when it was finished. Nothing escaped *her* minute observation and general curiosity; she saw everything, and asked everything; was never easy till she knew the price of every part of Marianne's dress; could have guessed the number of her gowns altogether with better judgment than Marianne herself, and was not without hopes of finding out before they parted how much her washing cost per week, and how much she had every year to spend upon herself. The impertinence of these kind of scrutinies, moreover, was generally concluded with a compliment, which, though meant as its douceur, was considered by Marianne as the greatest impertinence of all; for after undergoing an examination into the value and make of her gown, the colour of her shoes, and the arrangement of her hair, she was almost sure of being told, that upon 'her word she looked vastly smart, and she dared to say would make a great many conquests.'

With such encouragement as this was she dismissed, on the present occasion, to her brother's carriage; which they were ready to enter five minutes after it stopped at the door, a punctuality

not very agreeable to their sister-in-law, who had preceded them to the house of her acquaintance, and was there hoping for some delay on their part that might inconvenience either herself or her coachman.

The events of the evening were not very remarkable. The party, like other musical parties, comprehended a great many people who had real taste for the performance, and a great many more who had none at all ; and the performers themselves were, as usual, in their own estimation, and that of their immediate friends, the first private performers in England.

As Elinor was neither musical, nor affecting to be so, she made no scruple of turning away her eyes from the grand pianoforte whenever it suited her, and, unrestrained even by the presence of a harp and a violoncello, would fix them at pleasure on any other object in the room. In one of these excursive glances she perceived, among the group of young men, the very he who had given them a lecture on toothpick-cases at Gray's. She perceived him soon afterwards looking at herself, and speaking familiarly to her brother ; and had just determined to find out his name from the latter, when they both came towards her, and Mr. Dashwood introduced him to her as Mr. Robert Ferrars.

SENSE AND SENSIBILITY

He addressed her with easy civility, and twisted his head into a bow which assured her, as plainly as words could have done, that he was exactly the coxcomb she had heard him described to be by Lucy. Happy had it been for her if her regard for Edward had depended less on his own merit, than on the merit of his nearest relations. For then his brother's bow must have given the finishing stroke to what the ill-humour of his mother and sister would have begun. But while she wondered at the difference of the two young men, she did not find that the emptiness and conceit of the one put her at all out of charity with the modesty and worth of the other. Why they *were* different Robert explained to her himself in the course of a quarter of an hour's conversation; for, talking of his brother, and lamenting the extreme *gaucherie* which he really believed kept him from mixing in proper society, he candidly and generously attributed it much less to any natural deficiency, than to the misfortune of a private education; while he himself, though probably without any particular, any material superiority by nature, merely from the advantage of a public school, was as well fitted to mix in the world as any other man.

'Upon my soul,' he added, 'I believe it is nothing more : and so I often tell my mother when she is grieving about it. "My dear madam,"

I always say to her, "you must make yourself easy. The evil is now irremediable, and it has been entirely your own doing. Why would you be persuaded by my uncle, Sir Robert, against your own judgment, to place Edward under private tuition, at the most critical time of his life? If you had only sent him to Westminster as well as myself, instead of sending him to Mr. Pratt's, all this would have been prevented." This is the way in which I always consider the matter, and my mother is perfectly convinced of her error.'

Elinor would not oppose his opinion, because whatever might be her general estimation of the advantage of a public school, she could not think of Edward's abode in Mr. Pratt's family with any satisfaction.

'You reside in Devonshire, I think,' was his next observation, 'in a cottage near Dawlish.'

Elinor set him right as to its situation, and it seemed rather surprising to him that anybody could live in Devonshire without living near Dawlish. He bestowed his hearty approbation, however, on their species of house.

'For my own part,' said he, 'I am excessively fond of a cottage; there is always so much comfort, so much elegance about them. And I protest, if I had any money to spare, I should buy a little land and build one myself, within a short distance of London, where I might drive myself down at any time, and collect a few friends about me, and be happy. I advise everybody who is going to build, to build a cottage. My friend Lord Courtland came to me the other day on purpose to ask my advice, and laid before me three different plans of Bonomi's. I was to decide on the best of them. "My dear Courtland," said I, immediately throwing them all into the fire, "do not adopt either of them, but by all means build a cottage." And that, I fancy, will be the end of it.

'Some people imagine that there can be no accommodations, no space in a cottage; but this is all a mistake. I was last month at my friend Elliott's, near Dartford. Lady Elliott wished to give a dance. "But how can it be done?" said she; "my dear Ferrars, do tell me how it is to be managed. There is not a room in this cottage that will hold ten couple, and where can the supper be?" *I* immediately saw that there could be no difficulty in it, so I said, "My dear Lady Elliott, do not be uneasy. The dining-parlour will admit eighteen couple with ease; card-tables may be placed in the drawing-room; the library may be open for tea and other refreshments; and let the supper be set out in the saloon." Lady Elliott was delighted with the thought. We measured the dining-room, and found it would hold exactly eighteen couple, and the affair was arranged precisely after my plan. So that in fact, you see, if people do but know how to set about it, every comfort may be as well enjoyed in a cottage as in the most spacious dwelling.'

Elinor agreed to it all, for she did not think he deserved the compliment of rational opposition.

As John Dashwood had no more pleasure in music than his eldest sister, his mind was equally at liberty to fix on anything else ; and a thought struck him during the evening, which he communicated to his wife, for her approbation, when they got home. The consideration of Mrs. Dennison's mistake, in supposing his sisters their guests, had suggested the propriety of their being really invited to become such, while Mrs. Jennings's engagements kept her from home. The expense would be nothing, the inconvenience not more ; and it was altogether an attention which the delicacy of his conscience pointed out to be requisite to its complete enfranchisement from his promise to his father. Fanny was startled at the proposal.

'I do not see how it can be done,' said she, 'without affronting Lady Middleton, for they spend every day with her ; otherwise I should be exceedingly glad to do it. You know I am always ready to pay them any attention in my power, as my taking them out this evening shews. But they are Lady Middleton's visitors. How can I ask them away from her?'

Her husband, but with great humility, did not see the force of her objection. 'They had already spent a week in this manner in Conduit Street, and Lady Middleton could not be displeased at their giving the same number of days to such near relations.'

Fanny paused a moment, and then, with fresh vigour, said—

'My love, I would ask them with all my heart, if it was in my power. But I have just settled within myself to ask the Miss Steeles to spend a few days with us. They are very well-behaved, good kind of girls; and I think the attention is due to them, as their uncle did so very well by Edward. We can ask your sisters some other year, you know; but the Miss Steeles may not be in town any more. I am sure you will like them; indeed, you *do* like them, you know, very much already, and so does my mother; and they are such favourites with Harry!'

Mr. Dashwood was convinced. He saw the necessity of inviting the Miss Steeles immediately, and his conscience was pacified by the resolution of inviting his sisters another year; at the same time, however, slyly suspecting that another year would make the invitation needless, by bringing Elinor to town as Colonel Brandon's wife, and Marianne as *their* visitor.

Fanny, rejoicing in her escape, and proud of the ready wit that had procured it, wrote the next morning to Lucy, to request her company and her sister's for some days in Harley Street, as soon as Lady Middleton could spare them. This was enough to make Lucy really and reasonably happy. Mrs. Dashwood seemed actually working for her herself, cherishing all her hopes, and promoting all her views! Such an opportunity of being with Edward and his family was, above all things, the most material to her interest, and such an invitation the most gratifying to her feelings! It was an advantage that could not be too gratefully acknowledged, nor too speedily made use of; and the visit to Lady Middleton, which had not before had any precise limits, was instantly discovered to have been always meant to end in two days' time.

When the note was shewn to Elinor, as it was within ten minutes after its arrival, it gave her, for the first time, some share in the expectations of Lucy; for such a mark of uncommon kindness, vouchsafed on so short an acquaintance, seemed to declare that the goodwill towards her arose from something more than merely malice against herself, and might be

94

brought, by time and address, to do everything
that Lucy wished. Her flattery had already
subdued the pride of Lady Middleton, and
made an entry into the close heart of Mrs. John
Dashwood; and these were effects that laid
open the probability of greater.

The Miss Steeles removed to Harley Street,
and all that reached Elinor of their influence
there strengthened her expectation of the event.
Sir John, who called on them more than once,
brought home such accounts of the favour they
were in as must be universally striking. Mrs.
Dashwood had never been so much pleased with
any young women in her life as she was with
them; had given each of them a needle-book,
made by some emigrant; called Lucy by her
Christian name; and did not know whether she
should ever be able to part with them.

CHAPTER XXXVII

Mrs. Palmer was so well at the end of a fort-night that her mother felt it no longer necessary to give up the whole of her time to her; and, contenting herself with visiting her once or twice a day, returned from that period to her own home, and her own habits, in which she found the Miss Dashwoods very ready to re-assume their former share.

About the third or fourth morning after their being thus resettled in Berkeley Street, Mrs. Jennings, on returning from her ordinary visit to Mrs. Palmer, entered the drawing-room, where Elinor was sitting by herself, with an air of such hurrying importance as prepared her to hear something wonderful; and, giving her time only to form that idea, began directly to justify it by saying—

'Lord! my dear Miss Dashwood! have you heard the news?'

'No, ma'am. What is it?'

'Something so strange! But you shall hear it all. When I got to Mr. Palmer's, I found

Charlotte quite in a fuss about the child. She was sure it was very ill—it cried, and fretted, and was all over pimples. So I looked at it directly, and, "Lord! my dear," says I, "it is nothing in the world but the red-gum"; and nurse said just the same. But Charlotte, she would not be satisfied, so Mr. Donavan was sent for; and luckily he happened to be just come in from Harley Street, so he stepped over directly, and as soon as ever he saw the child he said just as we did, that it was nothing in the world but the red-gum, and then Charlotte was easy. And so, just as he was going away again, it came into my head, I am sure I do not know how I happened to think of it, but it came into my head to ask him if there was any news. So upon that he smirked, and simpered, and looked grave, and seemed to know something or other, and at last he said in a whisper, "For fear any unpleasant report should reach the young ladies under your care as to their sister's indisposition, I think it advisable to say that I believe there is no great reason for alarm; I hope Mrs. Dashwood will do very well."'

'What! is Fanny ill?'

'That is exactly what I said, my dear. "Lord!" says I, "is Mrs. Dashwood ill?" So then it all came out; and the long and the short of the matter, by all I can learn, seems to be

this:—Mr. Edward Ferrars, the very young man
I used to joke with you about (but however, as
it turns out, I am monstrous glad there never
was anything in it), Mr. Edward Ferrars, it
seems, has been engaged above this twelvemonth
to my cousin Lucy! There's for you, my dear!
And not a creature knowing a syllable of the
matter except Nancy! Could you have believed
such a thing possible? There is no great wonder
in their liking one another; but that matters
should be brought so forward between them,
and nobody suspect it! *That* is strange! I
never happened to see them together, or I am
sure I should have found it out directly. Well,
and so this was kept a great secret, for fear of
Mrs. Ferrars; and neither she nor your brother
or sister suspected a word of the matter—till
this very morning, poor Nancy, who, you know,
is a well-meaning creature, but no conjuror,
popt it all out. "Lord!" thinks she to herself,
"they are all so fond of Lucy, to be sure they
will make no difficulty about it"; and so, away
she went to your sister, who was sitting all alone
at her carpet-work, little suspecting what was
to come—for she had just been saying to your
brother, only five minutes before, that she thought
to make a match between Edward and some
lord's daughter or other, I forget who. So you
may think what a blow it was to all her vanity

and pride. She fell into violent hysterics
immediately, with such screams as reached your
brother's ears, as he was sitting in his own dressing-room downstairs, thinking about writing a
letter to his steward in the country. So up
he flew directly, and a terrible scene took place,
for Lucy was come to them by that time, little
dreaming what was going on. Poor soul! I pity
her. And I must say, I think she was used very
hardly; for your sister scolded like any fury, and
soon drove her into a fainting fit. Nancy, she
fell upon her knees, and cried bitterly; and your
brother, he walked about the room, and said
he did not know what to do. Mrs. Dashwood
declared they should not stay a minute longer
in the house, and your brother was forced to go
down upon *his* knees too, to persuade her to let
them stay till they had packed up their clothes.
Then she fell into hysterics again, and he was so
frightened that he would send for Mr. Donavan,
and Mr. Donavan found the house in all this
uproar. The carriage was at the door ready to
take my poor cousins away, and they were just
stepping in as he came off; poor Lucy in such
a condition, he says, she could hardly walk; and
Nancy, she was almost as bad. I declare, I have
no patience with your sister; and I hope, with
all my heart, it will be a match in spite of her.
Lord! what a taking poor Mr. Edward will be

in when he hears of it! To have his love used so scornfully! for they say he is monstrous fond of her, as well he may. I should not wonder if he was to be in the greatest of a passion!—and Mr. Donavan thinks just the same. He and I had a great deal of talk about it; and the best of all is, that he is gone back again to Harley Street, that he may be within call when Mrs. Ferrars is told of it, for she was sent for as soon as ever my cousins left the house, for your sister was sure *she* would be in hysterics too; and so she may for what I care. I have no pity for either of them. I have no notion of people's making such a to-do about money and greatness. There is no reason on earth why Mr. Edward and Lucy should not marry; for I am sure Mrs. Ferrars may afford to do very well by her son; and though Lucy has next to nothing herself, she knows better than anybody how to make the most of everything; and I dare say, if Mrs. Ferrars would only allow him five hundred a year, she would make as good an appearance with it as anybody else would with eight. Lord! how snug they might live in such another cottage as yours—or a little bigger—with two maids and two men; and I believe I could help them to a housemaid, for my Betty has a sister out of place that would fit them exactly.'

Here Mrs. Jennings ceased; and as Elinor had

had time enough to collect her thoughts, she
was able to give such an answer, and make such
observations, as the subject might naturally be
supposed to produce. Happy to find that she
was not suspected of any extraordinary interest
in it; that Mrs. Jennings (as she had of late
often hoped might be the case) had ceased to
imagine her at all attached to Edward; and
happy, above all the rest, in the absence of
Marianne, she felt very well able to speak of the
affair without embarrassment, and to give her
judgment, as she believed with impartiality, on
the conduct of every one concerned in it.

She could hardly determine what her own
expectation of its event really was; though she
earnestly tried to drive away the notion of its
being possible to end otherwise at last than in
the marriage of Edward and Lucy. What Mrs.
Ferrars would say and do, though there could
not be a doubt of its nature, she was anxious
to hear; and still more anxious to know how
Edward would conduct himself. For *him* she
felt much compassion; for Lucy very little—
and it cost her some pains to procure that little;
—for the rest of the party none at all.

As Mrs. Jennings could talk on no other
subject, Elinor soon saw the necessity of preparing Marianne for its discussion. No time
was to be lost in undeceiving her, in making her

2 G*

acquainted with the real truth, and in endeavouring to bring her to hear it talked of by others, without betraying that she felt any uneasiness for her sister, or any resentment against Edward.

Elinor's office was a painful one. She was going to remove what she really believed to be her sister's chief consolation—to give such particulars of Edward as, she feared, would ruin him for ever in her good opinion—and to make Marianne, by a resemblance in their situations, which to *her* fancy would seem strong, feel all her own disappointment over again. But, unwelcome as such a task must be, it was necessary to be done, and Elinor therefore hastened to perform it.

She was very far from wishing to dwell on her own feelings, or to represent herself as suffering much, any otherwise than as the self-command she had practised since her first knowledge of Edward's engagement might suggest a hint of what was practicable to Marianne. Her narration was clear and simple; and though it could not be given without emotion, it was not accompanied by violent agitation nor impetuous grief. *That* belonged rather to the hearer, for Marianne listened with horror, and cried excessively. Elinor was to be the comforter of others in her own distresses no less than in theirs; and

all the comfort that could be given by assurances
of her own composure of mind, and a very earnest
vindication of Edward from every charge but of
imprudence, was readily offered.

But Marianne for some time would give
credit to neither. Edward seemed a second
Willoughby ; and acknowledging, as Elinor did,
that she *had* loved him most sincerely, could
she feel less than herself ! As for Lucy Steele,
she considered her so totally unamiable, so absolutely incapable of attaching a sensible man,
that she could not be persuaded at first to believe, and afterwards to pardon, any former
affection of Edward for her. She would not
even admit it to have been natural ; and Elinor
left her to be convinced that it was so, by that
which only could convince her, a better knowledge of mankind.

Her first communication had reached no
farther than to state the fact of the engagement, and the length of time it had existed.
Marianne's feelings had then broken in, and put
an end to all regularity of detail ; and for some
time all that could be done was to soothe her
distress, lessen her alarms, and combat her resentment. The first question on her side, which led
to farther particulars, was—

' How long has this been known to you,
Elinor ? Has he written to you ? '

'I have known it these four months. When Lucy first came to Barton Park last November, she told me in confidence of her engagement.'

At these words Marianne's eyes expressed the astonishment which her lips could not utter. After a pause of wonder, she exclaimed—

'Four months! Have you known of this four months?'

Elinor confirmed it.

'What!—while attending me in all my misery, has this been on your heart? and I have reproached you for being happy!'

'It was not fit that you should then know how much I was the reverse.'

'Four months!' cried Marianne again. 'So calm! so cheerful! How have you been supported?'

'By feeling that I was doing my duty. My promise to Lucy obliged me to be secret. I owed it to her, therefore, to avoid giving any hint of the truth ; and I owed it to my family and friends not to create in them a solicitude about me, which it could not be in my power to satisfy.'

Marianne seemed much struck.

'I have very often wished to undeceive yourself and my mother,' added Elinor ; 'and once or twice I have attempted it ;—but without betraying my trust I never could have convinced you.'

' Four months!—and yet you loved him!'

'Yes. But I did not love only him;—and while the comfort of others was dear to me, I was glad to spare them from knowing how much I felt. Now, I can think and speak of it with little emotion. I would not have you suffer on my account; for I assure you I no longer suffer materially myself. I have many things to support me. I am not conscious of having provoked the disappointment by any imprudence of my own, and I have borne it as much as possible without spreading it farther. I acquit Edward of all essential misconduct. I wish him very happy; and I am so sure of his always doing his duty, that though now he may harbour some regret, in the end he must become so. Lucy does not want sense, and that is the foundation on which everything good may be built. And after all, Marianne, after all that is bewitching in the idea of a single and constant attachment, and all that can be said of one's happiness depending entirely on any particular person, it is not meant—it is not fit—it is not possible that it should be so. Edward will marry Lucy; he will marry a woman superior in person and understanding to half her sex; and time and habit will teach him to forget that he ever thought another superior to *her*.'

'If such is your way of thinking,' said

Marianne, 'if the loss of what is most valued is so easily to be made up by something else, your resolution, your self-command, are perhaps a little less to be wondered at. They are brought more within my comprehension.'

'I understand you. You do not suppose that I have ever felt much. For four months, Marianne, I have had all this hanging on my mind, without being at liberty to speak of it to a single creature; knowing that it would make you and my mother most unhappy whenever it were explained to you, yet unable to prepare you for it in the least. It was told me—it was in a manner forced on me—by the very person herself whose prior engagement ruined all my prospects; and told me, as I thought, with triumph. This person's suspicions, therefore, I have had to oppose, by endeavouring to appear indifferent where I have been most deeply interested. And it has not been only once; I have had her hopes and exultation to listen to again and again. I have known myself to be divided from Edward for ever, without hearing one circumstance that could make me less desire the connexion. Nothing has proved him unworthy; nor has anything declared him indifferent to me. I have had to contend against the unkindness of his sister, and the insolence of his mother, and have suffered the punishment of an attachment without enjoying its advantages. And all this has been going on at a time when, as you too well know, it has not been my only unhappiness. If you can think me capable of ever feeling, surely you may suppose that I have suffered *now*. The composure of mind with which I have brought myself at present to consider the matter, the consolation that I have been willing to admit, have been the effect of constant and painful exertion ;—they did not spring up of themselves; they did not occur to relieve my spirits at first —no, Marianne. *Then*, if I had not been bound to silence, perhaps nothing could have kept me entirely—not even what I owed to my dearest friends—from openly shewing that I was *very* unhappy.'

Marianne was quite subdued.

'Oh! Elinor,' she cried, 'you have made me hate myself for ever. How barbarous have I been to you!—you, who have been my only comfort, who have borne with me in all my misery, who have seemed to be only suffering for me! Is this my gratitude? Is this the only return I can make you? Because your merit cries out upon myself, I have been trying to do it away.'

The tenderest caresses followed this confession. In such a frame of mind as she was now in, Elinor had no difficulty in obtaining from her whatever promise she required; and, at her request, Marianne engaged never to speak of the affair to any one with the least appearance of bitterness; to meet Lucy without betraying the smallest increase of dislike to her; and even to see Edward himself, if chance should bring them together, without any diminution of her usual cordiality. These were great concessions, but where Marianne felt that she had injured, no reparation could be too much for her to make.

She performed her promise of being discreet to admiration. She attended to all that Mrs. Jennings had to say upon the subject with an unchanging complexion, dissented from her in nothing, and was heard three times to say, 'Yes, ma'am.' She listened to her praise of Lucy with only moving from one chair to another, and when Mrs. Jennings talked of Edward's affection, it cost her only a spasm in her throat. Such advances towards heroism in her sister made Elinor feel equal to anything herself.

The next morning brought a farther trial of it, in a visit from their brother, who came with a most serious aspect to talk over the dreadful affair, and bring them news of his wife.

'You have heard, I suppose,' said he, with great solemnity, as soon as he was seated, 'of the very shocking discovery that took place under our roof yesterday.'

They all looked their assent; it seemed too awful a moment for speech.

'Your sister,' he continued, 'has suffered dreadfully. Mrs. Ferrars too—in short, it has been a scene of such complicated distress; but I will hope that the storm may be weathered without our being, any of us, quite overcome. Poor Fanny! she was in hysterics all yesterday. But I would not alarm you too much. Donavan says there is nothing materially to be apprehended; her constitution is a good one, and her resolution equal to anything. She has borne it all with the fortitude of an angel! She says she never shall think well of anybody again; and one cannot wonder at it, after being so deceived!—meeting with such ingratitude, where so much kindness had been shewn, so much confidence had been placed. It was quite out of the benevolence of her heart that she had asked these young women to her house; merely because she thought they deserved some attention, were harmless, well-behaved girls, and would be pleasant companions; for otherwise we both wished very much to have invited you and Marianne to be with us, while your kind friend there was attending her daughter. And now to be so rewarded! "I wish with all my heart," says poor Fanny, in her affectionate way, "that we had asked your sisters instead of them."'

Here he stopped to be thanked; which being done, he went on.

'What poor Mrs. Ferrars suffered, when first Fanny broke it to her, is not to be described. While she, with the truest affection, had been planning a most eligible connexion for him, was it to be supposed that he could be all the time secretly engaged to another person!—such a suspicion could never have entered her head! If she suspected *any* prepossession elsewhere, it could not be in *that* quarter. "*There*, to be sure," said she, "I might have thought myself safe." She was quite in an agony. We consulted together, however, as to what should be done, and at last she determined to send for Edward. He came. But I am sorry to relate what ensued. All that Mrs. Ferrars could say to make him put an end to the engagement, assisted, too, as you may well suppose, by my arguments, and Fanny's entreaties, was of no avail. Duty, affection, everything was disregarded. I never thought Edward so stubborn, so unfeeling, before. His mother explained to him her liberal designs, in case of his marrying Miss Morton; told him she would settle on him the Norfolk estate, which, clear of land-tax, brings in a good thousand a year; offered even, when matters grew desperate, to make it twelve hundred; and in opposition to this, if he still persisted in this low connexion, represented to him the certain penury that must attend the match. His own two thousand pounds, she protested, should be his all; she would never see him again; and so far would she be from affording him the smallest assistance, that if he were to enter into any profession with a view of better support, she would do all in her power to prevent his advancing in it.'

Here Marianne, in an ecstasy of indignation, clapped her hands together and cried, 'Gracious God! can this be possible!'

'Well may you wonder, Marianne,' replied her brother, 'at the obstinacy which could resist such arguments as these. Your exclamation is very natural.'

Marianne was going to retort, but she remembered her promises, and forbore.

'All this, however,' he continued, 'was urged in vain. Edward said very little; but what he did say was in the most determined manner. Nothing could prevail on him to give up his engagement. He would stand to it, cost him what it might.'

'Then,' cried Mrs. Jennings, with blunt sincerity, no longer able to be silent, 'he has acted

like an honest man. I beg your pardon, Mr.
Dashwood, but if he had done otherwise, I
should have thought him a rascal. I have some
little concern in the business, as well as yourself, for Lucy Steele is my cousin, and I believe there is not a better kind of girl in the
world, nor one who more deserves a good husband.'

John Dashwood was greatly astonished; but
his nature was calm, not open to provocation,
and he never wished to offend anybody, especially anybody of good fortune. He therefore
replied, without any resentment—

'I would by no means speak disrespectfully
of any relation of yours, madam. Miss Lucy
Steele is, I dare say, a very deserving young
woman, but in the present case, you know, the
connexion must be impossible. And to have
entered into a secret engagement with a young
man under her uncle's care, the son of a woman
especially of such very large fortune as Mrs.
Ferrars, is perhaps altogether a little extraordinary. In short, I do not mean to reflect
upon the behaviour of any person whom you
have a regard for, Mrs. Jennings. We all wish
her extremely happy, and Mrs. Ferrars's conduct throughout the whole has been such as
every conscientious, good mother, in like circumstances, would adopt. It has been dignified and

liberal. Edward has drawn his own lot, and I fear it will be a bad one.'

Marianne sighed out her similar apprehension; and Elinor's heart wrung for the feelings of Edward, while braving his mother's threats, for a woman who could not reward him.

'Well, sir,' said Mrs. Jennings, 'and how did it end?'

'I am sorry to say, ma'am, in a most unhappy rupture—Edward is dismissed for ever from his mother's notice. He left her house yesterday, but where he is gone, or whether he is still in town, I do not know; for *we*, of course, can make no inquiry.'

'Poor young man! and what is to become of him?'

'What indeed, ma'am! It is a melancholy consideration. Born to the prospect of such affluence! I cannot conceive a situation more deplorable. The interest of two thousand pounds —how can a man live on it! And when to that is added the recollection that he might, but for his own folly, within three months have been in receipt of two thousand five hundred a year (for Miss Morton has thirty thousand pounds), I cannot picture to myself a more wretched condition. We must all feel for him; and the more so, because it is totally out of our power to assist him.'

'Poor young man!' cried Mrs. Jennings, 'I am sure he should be very welcome to bed and board at my house; and so I would tell him, if I could see him. It is not fit that he should be living about at his own charge now, at lodgings and taverns.'

Elinor's heart thanked her for such kindness towards Edward, though she could not forbear smiling at the form of it.

'If he would only have done as well by himself,' said John Dashwood, 'as all his friends were disposed to do by him, he might now have been in his proper situation, and would have wanted for nothing. But as it is, it must be out of anybody's power to assist him. And there is one thing more preparing against him, which must be worse than all—his mother has determined, with a very natural kind of spirit, to settle *that* estate upon Robert immediately, which might have been Edward's on proper conditions. I left her this morning with her lawyer, talking over the business.'

'Well!' said Mrs. Jennings, 'that is *her* revenge. Everybody has a way of their own. But I don't think mine would be to make one son independent because another had plagued me.'

Marianne got up and walked about the room.

'Can anything be more galling to the spirit of

a man,' continued John, 'than to see his younger brother in possession of an estate which might have been his own? Poor Edward! I feel for him sincerely.'

A few minutes more, spent in the same kind of effusion, concluded his visit; and with repeated assurances to his sisters that he really believed there was no material danger in Fanny's indisposition, and that they need not therefore be very uneasy about it, he went away; leaving the three ladies unanimous in their sentiments on the present occasion, as far at least as it regarded Mrs. Ferrars's conduct, the Dashwoods', and Edward's.

Marianne's indignation burst forth as soon as he quitted the room; and as her vehemence made reserve impossible in Elinor, and unnecessary in Mrs. Jennings, they all joined in a very spirited critique upon the party.

CHAPTER XXXVIII

MRS. JENNINGS was very warm in her praise of
Edward's conduct, but only Elinor and Marianne
understood its true merit. *They* only knew
how little he had had to tempt him to be dis-
obedient, and how small was the consolation,
beyond the consciousness of doing right, that
could remain to him in the loss of friends and
fortune. Elinor gloried in his integrity; and
Marianne forgave all his offences in compassion
for his punishment. But though confidence
between them was, by this public discovery,
restored to its proper state, it was not a subject
on which either of them were fond of dwelling
when alone. Elinor avoided it upon principle,
as tending to fix still more upon her thoughts,
by the too warm, too positive assurances of
Marianne, that belief of Edward's continued
affection for herself, which she rather wished to
do away; and Marianne's courage soon failed
her, in trying to converse upon a topic which
always left her more dissatisfied with herself
than ever, by the comparison it necessarily

116

produced between Elinor's conduct and her own.

She felt all the force of that comparison; but not as her sister had hoped, to urge her to exertion now; she felt it with all the pain of continual self-reproach, regretted most bitterly that she had never exerted herself before; but it brought only the torture of penitence, without the hope of amendment. Her mind was so much weakened that she still fancied present exertion impossible, and therefore it only dispirited her more.

Nothing new was heard by them for a day or two afterwards of affairs in Harley Street or Bartlett's Buildings. But though so much of the matter was known to them already, that Mrs. Jennings might have had enough to do in spreading that knowledge farther, without seeking after more, she had resolved from the first to pay a visit of comfort and inquiry to her cousins as soon as she could; and nothing but the hindrance of more visitors than usual had prevented her going to them within that time.

The third day succeeding their knowledge of the particulars was so fine, so beautiful a Sunday as to draw many to Kensington Gardens, though it was only the second week in March. Mrs. Jennings and Elinor were of the number; but Marianne, who knew that the Willoughbys were again in town, and had a constant dread of meeting them, chose rather to stay at home than venture into so public a place.

An intimate acquaintance of Mrs. Jennings joined them soon after they entered the Gardens, and Elinor was not sorry that, by her continuing with them, and engaging all Mrs. Jennings's conversation, she was herself left to quiet reflection. She saw nothing of the Willoughbys, nothing of Edward, and for some time nothing of anybody who could by any chance, whether grave or gay, be interesting to her. But at last she found herself, with some surprise, accosted by Miss Steele, who, though looking rather shy, expressed great satisfaction in meeting them; and on receiving encouragement from the particular kindness of Mrs. Jennings, left her own party for a short time to join theirs. Mrs. Jennings immediately whispered to Elinor—

'Get it all out of her, my dear. She will tell you anything, if you ask. You see I cannot leave Mrs. Clarke.'

It was lucky, however, for Mrs. Jennings's curiosity, and Elinor's too, that she would tell anything *without* being asked, for nothing would otherwise have been learnt.

'I am so glad to see you,' said Miss Steele, taking her familiarly by the arm, 'for I wanted to see you, of all things in the world'; and then lowering her voice, 'I suppose Mrs. Jennings has heard all about it. Is she angry?'

'Not at all, I believe, with you.'

'That is a good thing. And Lady Middleton, is *she* angry?'

'I cannot suppose it possible that she should.'

'I am monstrous glad of it. Good gracious! I have had such a time of it! I never saw Lucy in such a rage in my life. She vowed at first she would never trim me up a new bonnet, nor do anything else for me again, so long as she lived; but now she is quite come to, and we are as good friends as ever. Look, she made me this bow to my hat, and put in the feather last night. There now, *you* are going to laugh at me too. But why should not I wear pink ribbons? I do not care if it *is* the doctor's favourite colour. I am sure, for my part, I should never have known he *did* like it better than any other colour, if he had not happened to say so. My cousins have been so plaguing me! I declare, sometimes, I do not know which way to look before them.'

She had wandered away to a subject on which Elinor had nothing to say, and therefore soon judged it expedient to find her way back again to the first.

'Well, but, Miss Dashwood,' speaking triumphantly, 'people may say what they chuse

about Mr. Ferrars's declaring he would not have
Lucy, for it's no such a thing, I can tell you;
and it's quite a shame for such ill-natured reports
to be spread abroad. Whatever Lucy might
think about it herself, you know it was no
business of other people to set it down for certain.'

'I never heard anything of the kind hinted
at before, I assure you,' said Elinor.

'Oh! did not you? But it *was* said, I know
very well, and by more than one; for Miss
Godby told Miss Sparks, that nobody in their
senses could expect Mr. Ferrars to give up a
woman like Miss Morton, with thirty thousand
pounds to her fortune, for Lucy Steele, that
had nothing at all; and I had it from Miss
Sparks myself. And besides that, my cousin
Richard said himself, that when it came to the
point, he was afraid Mr. Ferrars would be off;
and when Edward did not come near us for
three days, I could not tell what to think myself; and I believe in my heart Lucy gave it
all up for lost; for we came away from your
brother's Wednesday, and we saw nothing of
him not all Thursday, Friday, and Saturday,
and did not know what was become with him.
Once Lucy thought to write to him, but then
her spirit rose against that. However, this
morning he came, just as we came home from
church; and then it all came out, how he had

been sent for Wednesday to Harley Street,
and been talked to by his mother and all of
them, and how he had declared before them all
that he loved nobody but Lucy, and nobody but
Lucy would he have. And how he had been
so worried by what passed, that as soon as he
had went away from his mother's house, he had
got upon his horse, and rid into the country
somewhere or other; and how he had staid
about at an inn all Thursday and Friday, on
purpose to get the better of it. And after
thinking it all over and over again, he said it
seemed to him as if, now he had no fortune, and
no nothing at all, it would be quite unkind to
keep her on to the engagement, because it must
be for her loss, for he had nothing but two
thousand pounds, and no hope of anything else;
and if he was to go into orders, as he had some
thoughts, he could get nothing but a curacy,
and how was they to live upon that?—He could
not bear to think of her doing no better, and so
he begged, if she had the least mind for it, to
put an end to the matter directly, and leave
him to shift for himself. I heard him say all
this as plain as could possibly be. And it was
entirely for *her* sake, and upon *her* account, that
he said a word about being off, and not upon his
own. I will take my oath he never dropt a
syllable of being tired of her, or of wishing to

marry Miss Morton, or anything like it. But, to be sure, Lucy would not give ear to such kind of talking; so she told him directly (with a great deal about sweet and love, you know, and all that—Oh la! one can't repeat such kind of things, you know)—she told him directly, she had not the least mind in the world to be off, for she could live with him upon such a trifle, and how little soever he might have, she should be very glad to have it all, you know, or something of the kind. So then he was monstrous happy, and talked on some time about what they should do, and they agreed he should take orders directly, and they must wait to be married till he got a living. And just then I could not hear any more, for my cousin called from below to tell me Mrs. Richardson was come in her coach, and would take one of us to Kensington Gardens; so I was forced to go into the room and interrupt them, to ask Lucy if she would like to go, but she did not care to leave Edward; so I just run upstairs and put on a pair of silk stockings, and came off with the Richardsons.'

'I do not understand what you mean by interrupting them,' said Elinor; 'you were all in the same room together, were not you?'

'No indeed! not us. La! Miss Dashwood, do you think people make love when anybody else is by? Oh! for shame! To be sure, you must know better than that. (Laughing affectedly.)—No, no; they were shut up in the drawing-room together, and all I heard was only by listening at the door.'

'How!' cried Elinor; 'have you been repeating to me what you only learnt yourself by listening at the door? I am sorry I did not know it before; for I certainly would not have suffered you to give me particulars of a conversation which you ought not to have known yourself. How could you behave so unfairly by your sister?'

'Oh la! there is nothing in *that*. I only stood at the door, and heard what I could. And I am sure Lucy would have done just the same by me; for, a year or two back, when Martha Sharpe and I had so many secrets together, she never made any bones of hiding in a closet, or behind a chimney-board, on purpose to hear what we said.'

Elinor tried to talk of something else; but Miss Steele could not be kept beyond a couple of minutes from what was uppermost in her mind.

'Edward talks of going to Oxford soon,' said she; 'but now he is lodging at No. —, Pall Mall. What an ill-natured woman her mother is, an't she? And your brother and sister were not very kind! However, I shan't say anything against them to *you*; and to be sure they did send us home in their own chariot, which was more than I looked for. And for my part, I was all in a fright for fear your sister should ask us for the huswifes she had gave us a day or two before; but, however, nothing was said about them, and I took care to keep mine out of sight. Edward have got some business at Oxford, he says, so he must go there for a time; and after *that*, as soon as he can light upon a bishop, he will be ordained. I wonder what curacy he will get! Good gracious! (giggling as she spoke) I 'd lay my life I know what my cousins will say, when they hear of it. They will tell me I should write to the doctor, to get Edward the curacy of his new living. I know they will; but I am sure I would not do such a thing for all the world. "La!" I shall say directly, "I wonder how you could think of such a thing. *I* write to the doctor, indeed!"'

'Well,' said Elinor, 'it is a comfort to be prepared against the worst. You have got your answer ready.'

Miss Steele was going to reply on the same subject, but the approach of her own party made another more necessary.

'Oh la! here come the Richardsons. I had a vast deal more to say to you, but I must not stay away from them not any longer. I assure you they are very genteel people. He makes a monstrous deal of money, and they keep their own coach. I have not time to speak to Mrs. Jennings about it myself, but pray tell her I am quite happy to hear she is not in anger against us, and Lady Middleton the same; and if anything should happen to take you and your sister away, and Mrs. Jennings should want company, I am sure we should be very glad to come and stay with her for as long a time as she likes. I suppose Lady Middleton won't ask us any more this bout. Good-bye; I am sorry Miss Marianne was not here. Remember me kindly to her. La! if you have not got your best spotted muslin on!—I wonder you was not afraid of its being torn.'

Such was her parting concern; for after this she had time only to pay her farewell compliments to Mrs. Jennings, before her company was claimed by Mrs. Richardson: and Elinor was left in possession of knowledge which might feed her powers of reflection some time, though she had learnt very little more than what had been already foreseen and foreplanned in her own mind. Edward's marriage with Lucy was as firmly determined on, and the time of its taking place remained as absolutely uncertain, as she had concluded it would be; everything depended, exactly after her expectation, on his getting that preferment, of which, at present, there seemed not the smallest chance.

As soon as they returned to the carriage Mrs. Jennings was eager for information; but as Elinor wished to spread as little as possible intelligence that had in the first place been so unfairly obtained, she confined herself to the brief repetition of such simple particulars, as she felt assured that Lucy, for the sake of her own consequence, would chuse to have known. The continuance of their engagement, and the means that were to be taken for promoting its end, was all her communication; and this produced from Mrs. Jennings the following natural remark—

'Wait for his having a living!—ay, we all know how *that* will end;—they will wait a twelvemonth, and finding no good comes of it, will set down upon a curacy of fifty pounds a year, with the interest of his two thousand pounds, and what little matter Mr. Steele and Mr. Pratt can give her.—Then they will have a child every year! and Lord help 'em! how poor they will be! I must see what I can give them towards furnishing their house. Two maids and two men indeed!—as I talked of t'other day.—No, no, they must get a stout girl of all works.— Betty's sister would never do for them *now*.'

The next morning brought Elinor a letter by

the twopenny post from Lucy herself. It was as follows :—

'BARTLETT'S BUILDINGS, *March.*

'I hope my dear Miss Dashwood will excuse the liberty I take of writing to her; but I know your friendship for me will make you pleased to hear such a good account of myself and my dear Edward, after all the troubles we have went through lately, therefore will make no more apologies, but proceed to say that, thank God! though we have suffered dreadfully, we are both quite well now, and as happy as we must always be in one another's love. We have had great trials, and great persecutions, but, however, at the same time, gratefully acknowledge many friends, yourself not the least among them, whose great kindness I shall always thankfully remember, as will Edward too, who I have told of it. I am sure you will be glad to hear, as likewise dear Mrs. Jennings, I spent two happy hours with him yesterday afternoon, he would not hear of our parting, though earnestly did I, as I thought my duty required, urge him to it for prudence sake, and would have parted for ever on the spot, would he consent to it; but he said it should never be, he did not regard his mother's anger, while he could have my affections; our prospects are not very bright, to be sure, but we must wait, and hope for the best; he will be ordained shortly, and should it ever be in your power to recommend him to anybody that has a living to bestow, am very sure you will not forget us, and dear Mrs. Jennings too, trust she will break a good word for us to Sir John, or Mr. Palmer, or any friend that may be able to assist us.——Poor Anne was much to blame for what she did, but she did it for the best, so I say nothing; hope Mrs. Jennings won't think it too much trouble to give us a call, should she come this way any morning, 'twould be a great kind-ness, and my cousins would be proud to know her.——My paper reminds me to conclude, and begging to be most gratefully and respectfully remembered to her, and to Sir John and Lady Middleton, and the dear children, when you chance to see them, and love to Miss Marianne,

'I am, etc., etc.'

As soon as Elinor had finished it, she per-formed what she concluded to be its writer's real design, by placing it in the hands of Mrs. Jennings, who read it aloud with many comments of satisfaction and praise.

'Very well indeed!——how prettily she writes! ——ay, that was quite proper to let him be off if he would. That was just like Lucy.——Poor soul! I wish I *could* get him a living with all my heart.——She calls me dear Mrs. Jennings, you see. She is a good-hearted girl as ever lived. Very well, upon my word. That sentence is very prettily turned. Yes, yes, I will go and see her sure enough. How attentive she is, to think of everybody !—Thank you, my dear, for shewing it me. It is as pretty a letter as ever I saw, and does Lucy's head and heart great credit.'

CHAPTER XXXIX

THE Miss Dashwoods had now been rather more than two months in town, and Marianne's impatience to be gone increased every day. She sighed for the air, the liberty, the quiet of the country; and fancied that if any place could give her ease, Barton must do it. Elinor was hardly less anxious than herself for their removal, and only so much less bent on its being effected immediately, as that she was conscious of the difficulties of so long a journey, which Marianne could not be brought to acknowledge. She began, however, seriously to turn her thoughts towards its accomplishment, and had already mentioned their wishes to their kind hostess, who resisted them with all the eloquence of her goodwill, when a plan was suggested, which, though detaining them from home yet a few weeks longer, appeared to Elinor altogether much more eligible than any other. The Palmers were to remove to Cleveland about the end of March, for the Easter holidays; and Mrs. Jennings, with both her friends, received

a very warm invitation from Charlotte to go
with them. This would not, in itself, have
been sufficient for the delicacy of Miss Dashwood ;—but it was enforced with so much real
politeness by Mr. Palmer himself, as, joined to
the very great amendment of his manners towards them since her sister had been known
to be unhappy, induced her to accept it with
pleasure.

When she told Marianne what she had done,
however, her first reply was not very auspicious.

'Cleveland!' she cried, with great agitation.
'No, I cannot go to Cleveland.'

'You forget,' said Elinor gently, 'that its
situation is not . . . that it is not in the neigh-
bourhood of . . .'

'But it is in Somersetshire. I cannot go
into Somersetshire. There, where I looked
forward to going . . . No, Elinor, you cannot
expect me to go there.'

Elinor would not argue upon the propriety
of overcoming such feelings ;—she only endeavoured to counteract them by working on others ;
—and represented it, therefore, as a measure
which would fix the time of her returning to
that dear mother, whom she so much wished
to see, in a more eligible, more comfortable
manner, than any other plan could do, and
perhaps without any greater delay. From

131

Cleveland, which was within a few miles of Bristol, the distance to Barton was not beyond one day, though a long day's journey ; and their mother's servant might easily come there to attend them down ; and as there could be no occasion for their staying above a week at Cleveland, they might now be at home in little more than three weeks' time. As Marianne's affection for her mother was sincere, it must triumph, with little difficulty, over the imaginary evil she had started.

Mrs. Jennings was so far from being weary of her guests, that she pressed them very earnestly to return with her again from Cleveland. Elinor was grateful for the attention, but it could not alter their design ; and their mother's concurrence being readily gained, everything relative to their return was arranged as far as it could be ;—and Marianne found some relief in drawing up a statement of the hours that were yet to divide her from Barton.

'Ah ! Colonel, I do not know what you and I shall do without the Miss Dashwoods,' was Mrs. Jennings's address to him when he first called on her, after their leaving her was settled ; 'for they are quite resolved upon going home from the Palmers ;—and how forlorn we shall be, when I come back !—Lord ! we shall sit and gape at one another as dull as two cats.'

Perhaps Mrs. Jennings was in hopes, by this vigorous sketch of their future *ennui*, to provoke him to make that offer which might give himself an escape from it—and if so, she had soon afterwards good reason to think her object gained; for, on Elinor's moving to the window to take more expeditiously the dimensions of a print which she was going to copy for her friend, he followed her to it with a look of particular meaning, and conversed with her there for several minutes. The effect of this discourse on the lady, too, could not escape her observation; for though she was too honourable to listen, and had even changed her seat on purpose that she might *not* hear, to one close by the pianoforte on which Marianne was playing, she could not keep herself from seeing that Elinor changed colour, attended with agitation, and was too intent on what he said to pursue her employment. Still farther in confirmation of her hopes, in the interval of Marianne's turning from one lesson to another, some words of the Colonel's inevitably reached her ear, in which he seemed to be apologising for the badness of his house. This set the matter beyond a doubt. She wondered indeed at his thinking it necessary to do so; but supposed it to be the proper etiquette. What Elinor said in reply she could not distinguish, but judged from the motion of her lips that she did not think *that* any material objection;—and Mrs. Jennings commended her in her heart for being so honest. They then talked on for a few minutes longer without her catching a syllable, when another lucky stop in Marianne's performance brought her these words in the Colonel's calm voice—

'I am afraid it cannot take place very soon.'

Astonished and shocked at so unloverlike a speech, she was almost ready to cry out, 'Lord! what should hinder it!'—but checking her desire, confined herself to this silent ejaculation—

'This is very strange!—sure he need not wait to be older.'

This delay on the Colonel's side, however, did not seem to offend or mortify his fair companion in the least; for on their breaking up the conference soon afterwards, and moving different ways, Mrs. Jennings very plainly heard Elinor say, and in a voice which shewed her to feel what she said—

'I shall always think myself very much obliged to you.'

Mrs. Jennings was delighted with her gratitude, and only wondered that, after hearing such a sentence, the Colonel should be able to take leave of them, as he immediately did, with the utmost *sang-froid*, and go without making

her any reply!—She had not thought her old
friend could have made so indifferent a suitor.

What had really passed between them was to
this effect—

'I have heard,' said he, with great compassion,
'of the injustice your friend Mr. Ferrars has
suffered from his family; for, if I understand
the matter right, he has been entirely cast off
by them for persevering in his engagement with
a very deserving young woman. Have I been
rightly informed?—Is it so?'

Elinor told him that it was.

'The cruelty, the impolitic cruelty,' he replied,
with great feeling, 'of dividing, or attempting to
divide, two young people long attached to each
other, is terrible. Mrs. Ferrars does not know
what she may be doing—what she may drive
her son to. I have seen Mr. Ferrars two or
three times in Harley Street, and am much
pleased with him. He is not a young man with
whom one can be intimately acquainted in a
short time, but I have seen enough of him to
wish him well for his own sake, and as a friend
of yours, I wish it still more. I understand that
he intends to take orders. Will you be so good
as to tell him that the living of Delaford, now
just vacant, as I am informed by this day's post,
is his, if he think it worth his acceptance;—but
that, perhaps, so unfortunately circumstanced as

he is now, it may be nonsense to appear to doubt;
I only wish it were more valuable. It is a rectory,
but a small one ; the late incumbent, I believe,
did not make more than two hundred pounds
per annum; and though it is certainly capable of
improvement, I fear not to such an amount as
to afford him a very comfortable income. Such
as it is, however, my pleasure in presenting him
to it will be very great. Pray assure him of it.'

Elinor's astonishment at this commission could
hardly have been greater had the Colonel been
really making her an offer of his hand. The
preferment, which only two days before she had
considered as hopeless for Edward, was already
provided to enable him to marry ;—and *she*, of
all people in the world, was fixed on to bestow
it ! Her emotion was such as Mrs. Jennings
had attributed to a very different cause ;—but
whatever minor feelings less pure, less pleasing,
might have a share in that emotion, her esteem
for the general benevolence, and her gratitude
for the particular friendship, which together
prompted Colonel Brandon to this act, were
strongly felt, and warmly expressed. She
thanked him for it with all her heart, spoke of
Edward's principles and disposition with that
praise which she knew them to deserve, and
promised to undertake the commission with
pleasure, if it were really his wish to put off

so agreeable an office to another. But, at the same time, she could not help thinking that no one could so well perform it as himself. It was an office, in short, from which, unwilling to give Edward the pain of receiving an obligation from *her*, she would have been very glad to be spared herself;—but Colonel Brandon, on motives of equal delicacy declining it likewise, still seemed so desirous of its being given through her means, that she would not on any account make farther opposition. Edward, she believed, was still in town, and fortunately she had heard his address from Miss Steele. She could undertake, therefore, to inform him of it in the course of the day. After this had been settled, Colonel Brandon began to talk of his own advantage in securing so respectable and agreeable a neighbour; and *then* it was that he mentioned with regret, that the house was small and indifferent;—an evil which Elinor, as Mrs. Jennings had supposed her to do, made very light of, at least as far as regarded its size.

'The smallness of the house,' said she, 'I cannot imagine any inconvenience to them, for it will be in proportion to their family and income.'

By which the Colonel was surprised to find that *she* was considering their marriage as the certain consequence of the presentation; for he did not suppose it possible that Delaford living could supply such an income as anybody in their style of life would venture to settle on—and he said so.

'This little rectory *can* do no more than make Mr. Ferrars comfortable as a bachelor; it cannot enable him to marry. I am sorry to say that my patronage ends with this; and my interest is hardly more extensive. If, however, by any unforeseen chance it should be in my power to serve him farther, I must think very differently of him from what I now do, if I am not as ready to be useful to him then as I sincerely wish I could be at present. What I am now doing, indeed, seems nothing at all, since it can advance him so little towards what must be his principal, his only object of happiness. His marriage must still be a distant good;—at least I am afraid it cannot take place very soon.'

Such was the sentence which, when misunderstood, so justly offended the delicate feelings of Mrs. Jennings; but after this narration of what really passed between Colonel Brandon and Elinor, while they stood at the window, the gratitude expressed by the latter on their parting may perhaps appear, in general, not less reasonably excited, nor less properly worded, than if it had arisen from an offer of marriage.

CHAPTER XL

'WELL, Miss Dashwood,' said Mrs. Jennings, sagaciously smiling, as soon as the gentleman had withdrawn, 'I do not ask you what the Colonel has been saying to you; for though, upon my honour, I *tried* to keep out of hearing, I could not help catching enough to understand his business. And I assure you I never was better pleased in my life, and I wish you joy of it with all my heart.'

'Thank you, ma'am,' said Elinor. 'It *is* a matter of great joy to me; and I feel the goodness of Colonel Brandon most sensibly. There are not many men who would act as he has done. Few people have so compassionate a heart! I never was more astonished in my life.'

'Lord! my dear, you are very modest! I an't the least astonished at it in the world, for I have often thought, of late, there was nothing more likely to happen.'

'You judged from your knowledge of the Colonel's general benevolence; but at least you

139

could not foresee that the opportunity would so very soon occur.'

'Opportunity!' repeated Mrs. Jennings — 'Oh! as to that, when a man has once made up his mind to such a thing, somehow or other he will soon find an opportunity. Well, my dear, I wish you joy of it again and again; and if ever there was a happy couple in the world, I think I shall soon know where to look for them.'

'You mean to go to Delaford after them, I suppose,' said Elinor, with a faint smile.

'Ay, my dear, that I do indeed. And as to the house being a bad one, I do not know what the Colonel would be at, for it is as good a one as ever I saw.'

'He spoke of its being out of repair.'

'Well, and whose fault is that? Why don't he repair it?—who should do it but himself?'

They were interrupted by the servant's coming in, to announce the carriage being at the door; and Mrs. Jennings, immediately preparing to go, said—

'Well, my dear, I must be gone before I have had half my talk out. But, however, we may have it all over in the evening, for we shall be quite alone. I do not ask you to go with me, for I dare say your mind is too full of the matter to care for company; and beside, you must long to tell your sister all about it.'

140

Marianne had left the room before the conversation began. ·

'Certainly, ma'am, I shall tell Marianne of it; but I shall not mention it at present to anybody else.'

'Oh! very well,' said Mrs. Jennings, rather disappointed. 'Then you would not have me tell it Lucy, for I think of going as far as Holborn to-day.'

'No, ma'am, not even Lucy, if you please. One day's delay will not be very material; and till I have written to Mr. Ferrars, I think it ought not to be mentioned to anybody else. I shall do *that* directly. It is of importance that no time should be lost with him, for he will, of course, have much to do relative to his ordination.'

This speech at first puzzled Mrs. Jennings exceedingly. Why Mr. Ferrars was to be written to about it in such a hurry she could not immediately comprehend. A few moments' reflection, however, produced a very happy idea, and she exclaimed—

'Oh ho! I understand you. Mr. Ferrars is to be the man. Well, so much the better for him. Ay, to be sure, he must be ordained in readiness; and I am very glad to find things are so forward between you. But, my dear, is not this rather out of character? Should not the

Colonel write himself? Sure, he is the proper person.'

Elinor did not quite understand the beginning of Mrs. Jennings's speech; neither did she think it worth inquiring into; and therefore only replied to its conclusion.

'Colonel Brandon is so delicate a man, that he rather wished any one to announce his intentions to Mr. Ferrars than himself.'

'And so *you* are forced to do it. Well, *that* is an odd kind of delicacy! However, I will not disturb you (seeing her preparing to write). You know your own concerns best. So good-bye, my dear. I have not heard of anything to please me so well since Charlotte was brought to bed.'

And away she went, but returning again in a moment—

'I have just been thinking of Betty's sister, my dear. I should be very glad to get her so good a mistress. But whether she would do for a lady's maid, I am sure I can't tell. She is an excellent housemaid, and works very well at her needle. However, you will think of all that at your leisure.'

'Certainly, ma'am,' replied Elinor, not hearing much of what she said, and more anxious to be alone than to be mistress of the subject.

How she should begin—how she should

142

express herself in her note to Edward was now all her concern. The particular circumstances between them made a difficulty of that which to any other person would have been the easiest thing in the world; but she equally feared to say too much or too little, and sat deliberating over her paper, with the pen in her hand, till broken in on by the entrance of Edward himself.

He had met Mrs. Jennings at the door, in her way to the carriage, as he came to leave his farewell card; and she, after apologising for not returning herself, had obliged him to enter by saying that Miss Dashwood was above, and wanted to speak with him on very particular business.

Elinor had just been congratulating herself, in the midst of her perplexity, that however difficult it might be to express herself properly by letter, it was at least preferable to giving the information by word of mouth, when her visitor entered, to force her upon this greatest exertion of all. Her astonishment and confusion were very great on his so sudden appearance. She had not seen him before since his engagement became public, and therefore not since his knowing her to be acquainted with it; which, with the consciousness of what she had been thinking of, and what she had to tell him, made

her feel particularly uncomfortable for some
minutes. He too was much distressed, and they
sat down together in a most promising state of
embarrassment.—Whether he had asked her
pardon for his intrusion on first coming into the
room, he could not recollect; but determining
to be on the safe side, he made his apology in
form as soon as he could say anything, after
taking a chair.

'Mrs. Jennings told me,' said he, 'that you
wished to speak with me, at least I understood
her so—or I certainly should not have intruded
on you in such a manner; though, at the same
time, I should have been extremely sorry to
leave London without seeing you and your
sister; especially as it will most likely be some
time—it is not probable that I should soon
have the pleasure of meeting you again. I go
to Oxford to-morrow.'

'You would not have gone, however,' said
Elinor, recovering herself, and determined to
get over what she so much dreaded as soon as
possible, 'without receiving our good wishes,
even if we had not been able to give them in
person. Mrs. Jennings was quite right in what
she said. I have something of consequence to
inform you of, which I was on the point of
communicating by paper. I am charged with
a most agreeable office (breathing rather faster

than usual as she spoke). Colonel Brandon, who was here only ten minutes ago, has desired me to say, that, understanding you mean to take orders, he has great pleasure in offering you the living of Delaford, now just vacant, and only wishes it were more valuable. Allow me to congratulate you on having so respectable and well-judging a friend, and to join in his wish that the living—it is about two hundred a year —were much more considerable, and such as might better enable you to—as might be more than a temporary accommodation to yourself— such, in short, as might establish all your views of happiness.'

What Edward felt, as he could not say it himself, it cannot be expected that any one else should say it for him. He *looked* all the astonishment which such unexpected, which such unthought-of information could not fail of exciting; but he said only these two words—

'Colonel Brandon!'

'Yes,' continued Elinor, gathering more resolution as some of the worst was over, 'Colonel Brandon means it as a testimony of his concern for what has lately passed—for the cruel situation in which the unjustifiable conduct of your family has placed you—a concern which, I am sure, Marianne, myself, and all your friends must share; and likewise as a proof of his high

2 K   145

esteem for your general character, and his particular approbation of your behaviour on the present occasion.'

'Colonel Brandon give *me* a living! Can it be possible?'

'The unkindness of your own relations has made you astonished to find friendship anywhere.'

'No,' replied he, with sudden consciousness, 'not to find it in *you*; for I cannot be ignorant that to you, to your goodness, I owe it all. I feel it—I would express it if I could—but, as you well know, I am no orator.'

'You are very much mistaken. I do assure you that you owe it entirely, at least almost entirely, to your own merit, and Colonel Brandon's discernment of it. I have had no hand in it. I did not even know, till I understood his design, that the living was vacant; nor had it ever occurred to me that he might have such a living in his gift. As a friend of mine, of my family, he may perhaps—indeed I know he *has*, still greater pleasure in bestowing it; but, upon my word, you owe nothing to my solicitation.'

Truth obliged her to acknowledge some small share in the action; but she was at the same time so unwilling to appear as the benefactress of Edward, that she acknowledged it with hesitation; which probably contributed to fix that suspicion in his mind which had recently entered it. For a short time he sat deep in thought, after Elinor had ceased to speak; at last, as if it were rather an effort, he said—

'Colonel Brandon seems a man of great worth and respectability. I have always heard him spoken of as such, and your brother, I know, esteems him highly. He is undoubtedly a sensible man, and in his manners perfectly the gentleman.'

'Indeed,' replied Elinor, 'I believe that you will find him, on farther acquaintance, all that you have heard him to be; and as you will be such very near neighbours (for I understand the parsonage is almost close to the mansion-house), it is particularly important that he *should* be all this.'

Edward made no answer; but when she had turned away her head, gave her a look, so serious, so earnest, so uncheerful, as seemed to say, that he might hereafter wish the distance between the parsonage and the mansion-house much greater.

'Colonel Brandon, I think, lodges in St. James's Street,' said he, soon afterwards, rising from his chair.

Elinor told him the number of the house.

'I must hurry away, then, to give him those
thanks which you will not allow me to give
you; to assure him that he has made me a very
—an exceedingly happy man.'

Elinor did not offer to detain him; and they
parted, with a very earnest assurance on *her* side
of her unceasing good wishes for his happiness
in every change of situation that might befall
him; on *his*, with rather an attempt to return
the same goodwill, than the power of express-
ing it.

'When I see him again,' said Elinor to
herself, as the door shut him out, 'I shall see
him the husband of Lucy.'

And with this pleasing anticipation she sat
down to reconsider the past, recall the words,
and endeavour to comprehend all the feelings of
Edward; and, of course, to reflect on her own
with discontent.

When Mrs. Jennings came home, though she
returned from seeing people whom she had never
seen before, and of whom therefore she must
have a great deal to say, her mind was so much
more occupied by the important secret in her
possession, than by anything else, that she
reverted to it again as soon as Elinor appeared.

'Well, my dear,' she cried, 'I sent you up
the young man. Did not I do right? And I
suppose you had no great difficulty.—You did

not find him very unwilling to accept your proposal?'

'No, ma'am; *that* was not very likely.'

'Well, and how soon will he be ready?—For it seems all to depend upon that.'

'Really,' said Elinor, 'I know so little of these kind of forms, that I can hardly even conjecture as to the time, or the preparation necessary; but I suppose two or three months will complete his ordination.'

'Two or three months!' cried Mrs. Jennings; 'Lord! my dear, how calmly you talk of it! and can the Colonel wait two or three months! Lord bless me!—I am sure it would put *me* quite out of patience. And though one would be very glad to do a kindness by poor Mr. Ferrars, I do think it is not worth while to wait two or three months for him. Sure, somebody else might be found that would do as well—somebody that is in orders already.'

'My dear ma'am,' said Elinor, 'what can you be thinking of?—Why, Colonel Brandon's only object is to be of use to Mr. Ferrars.'

'Lord bless you, my dear!—Sure you do not mean to persuade me that the Colonel only marries you for the sake of giving ten guineas to Mr. Ferrars!'

The deception could not continue after this; and an explanation immediately took place, by

2 K*

which both gained considerable amusement for
the moment, without any material loss of happiness to either, for Mrs. Jennings only exchanged
one form of delight for another, and still without forfeiting her expectation of the first.

'Ay, ay, the parsonage is but a small one,'
said she, after the first ebullition of surprise
and satisfaction was over, 'and very likely *may*
be out of repair; but to hear a man apologising,
as I thought, for a house that to my knowledge
has five sitting-rooms on the ground floor, and,
I think the housekeeper told me, could make
up fifteen beds!—And to you too, that had been
used to live in Barton Cottage! It seemed
quite ridiculous. But, my dear, we must touch
up the Colonel to do something to the parsonage,
and make it comfortable for them, before Lucy
goes to it.'

'But Colonel Brandon does not seem to have
any idea of the living's being enough to allow
them to marry.'

'The Colonel is a ninny, my dear; because he
has two thousand a year himself, he thinks that
nobody else can marry on less. Take my word
for it, that if I am alive, I shall be paying a
visit at Delaford Parsonage before Michaelmas;
and I am sure I shan't go if Lucy an't there.'

Elinor was quite of her opinion, as to the probability of their not waiting for anything more.

150

CHAPTER XLI

EDWARD, having carried his thanks to Colonel Brandon, proceeded with his happiness to Lucy; and such was the excess of it by the time he reached Bartlett's Buildings, that she was able to assure Mrs. Jennings, who called on her again the next day with her congratulations, that she had never seen him in such spirits before in her life.

Her own happiness, and her own spirits, were at least very certain; and she joined Mrs. Jennings most heartily in her expectation of their being all comfortably together in Delaford Parsonage before Michaelmas. So far was she, at the same time, from any backwardness to give Elinor that credit which Edward *would* give her, that she spoke of her friendship for them both with the most grateful warmth, was ready to own all their obligation to her, and openly declared that no exertion for their good on Miss Dashwood's part, either present or future, would ever surprise her, for she believed her capable of doing anything in the world for those she really valued. As for Colonel Brandon, she was not only ready to worship him as a saint, but was moreover truly anxious that he should be treated as one in all worldly concerns; anxious that his tithes should be raised to the utmost; and secretly resolved to avail herself at Delaford, as far as she possibly could, of his servants, his carriage, his cows, and his poultry.

It was now above a week since John Dashwood had called in Berkeley Street, and as since that time no notice had been taken by them of his wife's indisposition, beyond one verbal inquiry, Elinor began to feel it necessary to pay her a visit. This was an obligation, however, which not only opposed her own inclination, but which had not the assistance of any encouragement from her companions. Marianne, not contented with absolutely refusing to go herself, was very urgent to prevent her sister's going at all; and Mrs. Jennings, though her carriage was always at Elinor's service, so very much disliked Mrs. John Dashwood, that not even her curiosity to see how she looked after the late discovery, nor her strong desire to affront her by taking Edward's part, could overcome her unwillingness to be in her company again. The consequence was, that Elinor set out by herself to pay a visit, for which no one could really have less inclination, and to run the risk of a *tête-à-tête* with a woman whom neither of the others had so much reason to dislike.

Mrs. Dashwood was denied; but before the carriage could turn from the house her husband accidentally came out. He expressed great pleasure in meeting Elinor, told her that he had been just going to call in Berkeley Street, and assuring her that Fanny would be very glad to see her, invited her to come in.

They walked up stairs into the drawing-room. Nobody was there.

'Fanny is in her own room, I suppose,' said he;—'I will go to her presently, for I am sure she will not have the least objection in the world to seeing *you*—very far from it indeed. *Now* especially there cannot be—but, however, you and Marianne were always great favourites. Why would not Marianne come?'

Elinor made what excuse she could for her.

'I am not sorry to see you alone,' he replied, 'for I have a good deal to say to you. This living of Colonel Brandon's—can it be true? —has he really given it to Edward? I heard it yesterday by chance, and was coming to you on purpose to inquire farther about it.'

'It is perfectly true.—Colonel Brandon has given the living of Delaford to Edward.'

'Really!—Well, this is very astonishing!—no

relationship !—no connexion between them !—
and now that livings fetch such a price !—what
was the value of this ? '

' About two hundred a year.'

' Very well ; and for the next presentation to
a living of that value—supposing the late incumbent to have been old and sickly, and likely
to vacate it soon—he might have got, I dare
say, fourteen hundred pounds. And how came
he not to have settled that matter before this
person's death ?—*Now* indeed it would be too
late to sell it, but a man of Colonel Brandon's
sense !—I wonder he should be so improvident
in a point of such common, such natural concern ! Well, I am convinced that there is a
vast deal of inconsistency in almost every human
character. I suppose, however—on recollection
—that the case may probably be *this*. Edward
is only to hold the living till the person to whom
the Colonel has really sold the presentation is
old enough to take it.—Ay, ay, that is the
fact, depend upon it.'

Elinor contradicted it, however, very positively ; and by relating that she had herself
been employed in conveying the offer from
Colonel Brandon to Edward, and therefore must
understand the terms on which it was given,
obliged him to submit to her authority.

' It is truly astonishing ! ' he cried, after hear-

ing what she said. 'What could be the Colonel's
motive?'

'A very simple one—to be of use to Mr.
Ferrars.'

'Well, well; whatever Colonel Brandon may
be, Edward is a very lucky man! You will not
mention the matter to Fanny, however; for
though I have broke it to her, and she bears it
vastly well, she will not like to hear it much
talked of.'

Elinor had some difficulty here to refrain from
observing, that she thought Fanny might have
borne with composure an acquisition of wealth
to her brother, by which neither she nor her
child could be possibly impoverished.

'Mrs. Ferrars,' added he, lowering his voice
to the tone becoming so important a subject,
'knows nothing about it at present, and I believe it will be best to keep it entirely concealed
from her as long as may be.—When the marriage takes place, I fear she must hear of it all.'

'But why should such precaution be used?
Though it is not to be supposed that Mrs.
Ferrars can have the smallest satisfaction in
knowing that her son has money enough to live
upon—for *that* must be quite out of the question; yet why, after her late behaviour, is she
supposed to feel at all? She has done with her
son, she has cast him off for ever, and has made

all those over whom she had any influence cast him off likewise. Surely, after doing so, she cannot be imagined liable to any impression of sorrow or of joy on his account—she cannot be interested in anything that befalls him. She would not be so weak as to throw away the comfort of a child, and yet retain the anxiety of a parent!'

'Ah! Elinor,' said John, 'your reasoning is very good, but it is founded on ignorance of human nature. When Edward's unhappy match takes place, depend upon it his mother will feel as much as if she had never discarded him; and, therefore, every circumstance that may accelerate that dreadful event must be concealed from her as much as possible. Mrs. Ferrars can never forget that Edward is her son.'

'You surprise me; I should think it must nearly have escaped her memory by *this* time.'

'You wrong her exceedingly. Mrs. Ferrars is one of the most affectionate mothers in the world.'

Elinor was silent.

'We think *now*,' said Mr. Dashwood, after a short pause, 'of *Robert's* marrying Miss Morton.'

Elinor, smiling at the grave and decisive importance of her brother's tone, calmly replied—

'The lady, I suppose, has no choice in the affair.'

'Choice!—how do you mean?'

'I only mean, that I suppose from your manner of speaking, it must be the same to Miss Morton whether she marry Edward or Robert.'

'Certainly, there can be no difference; for Robert will now, to all intents and purposes, be considered as the eldest son; and as to anything else, they are both very agreeable young men—I do not know that one is superior to the other.'

Elinor said no more, and John was also for a short time silent. His reflections ended thus—

'Of *one* thing, my dear sister,' kindly taking her hand, and speaking in an awful whisper, 'I may assure you: and I *will* do it, because I know it must gratify you. I have good reason to think—indeed I have it from the best authority, or I should not repeat it, for otherwise it would be very wrong to say anything about it—but I have it from the very best authority—not that I ever precisely heard Mrs. Ferrars say it herself, but her daughter *did*, and I have it from her— that, in short, whatever objections there might be against a certain—a certain connexion—you understand me—it would have been far preferable to her, it would not have given her half the vexation that *this* does. I was exceedingly pleased to hear that Mrs. Ferrars considered it in that light—a very gratifying circumstance, you know, to us all. "It would have been beyond comparison," she said, "the least evil of the two, and she would be glad to compound *now* for nothing worse." But, however, all that is quite out of the question—not to be thought of or mentioned; as to any attachment, you know—it never could be—all that is gone by. But I thought I would just tell you of this, because I knew how much it must please you. Not that you have any reason to regret, my dear Elinor. There is no doubt of your doing exceedingly well—quite as well, or better, perhaps, all things considered. Has Colonel Brandon been with you lately?'

Elinor had heard enough, if not to gratify her vanity and raise her self-importance, to agitate her nerves and fill her mind; and she was therefore glad to be spared from the necessity of saying much in reply herself, and from the danger of hearing anything more from her brother, by the entrance of Mr. Robert Ferrars. After a few moments' chat, John Dashwood, recollecting that Fanny was yet uninformed of his sister being there, quitted the room in quest of her; and Elinor was left to improve her acquaintance with Robert, who, by the gay unconcern, the happy self-complacency of his manner while enjoying so unfair a division of his mother's love and liberality, to the prejudice of his banished brother, earned only by his own dissipated course of life, and that brother's integrity, was confirming her most unfavourable opinion of his head and heart.

They had scarcely been two minutes by themselves before he began to speak of Edward; for he too had heard of the living, and was very inquisitive on the subject. Elinor repeated the particulars of it, as she had given them to John, and their effect on Robert, though very different, was not less striking than it had been on *him*. He laughed most immoderately. The idea of Edward's being a clergyman, and living in a small parsonage-house, diverted him beyond measure; and when to that was added the fanciful imagery of Edward reading prayers in a white surplice, and publishing the banns of marriage between John Smith and Mary Brown, he could conceive nothing more ridiculous.

Elinor, while she waited in silence and immovable gravity the conclusion of such folly, could not restrain her eyes from being fixed on him with a look that spoke all the contempt it excited. It was a look, however, very well bestowed, for it relieved her own feelings, and gave no intelligence to him. He was recalled from wit to wisdom, not by any reproof of hers, but by his own sensibility.

'We may treat it as a joke,' said he at last, recovering from the affected laugh which had considerably lengthened out the genuine gaiety of the moment; 'but, upon my soul, it is a most serious business. Poor Edward! he is ruined for ever. I am extremely sorry for it—for I know him to be a very good-hearted creature; as well-meaning a fellow, perhaps, as any in the world. You must not judge of him, Miss Dashwood, from *your* slight acquaintance. Poor Edward! His manners are certainly not the happiest in nature. But we are not all born, you know, with the same powers—the same address. Poor fellow! to see him in a circle of strangers!—to be sure it was pitiable enough!—but, upon my soul, I believe he has as good a heart as any in the kingdom; and I declare and protest to you I never was so shocked in my life as when it all burst forth. I could not believe it. My mother was the first person who told me of it, and I, feeling myself called on to act with resolution, immediately said to her, "My dear madam, I do not know what you may intend to do on the occasion, but as for myself, I must say, that if Edward does marry this young woman, *I* never will see him again." That was what I said immediately—

I was most uncommonly shocked indeed! Poor
Edward! he has done for himself completely!
—shut himself out for ever from all decent
society!—but, as I directly said to my mother,
I am not in the least surprised at it; from his
style of education it was always to be expected.
My poor mother was half frantic.'

'Have you ever seen the lady?'

'Yes, once; while she was staying in this
house. I happened to drop in for ten minutes;
and I saw quite enough of her. The merest
awkward country girl, without style or elegance,
and almost without beauty. I remember her
perfectly. Just the kind of girl I should suppose likely to captivate poor Edward. I offered
immediately, as soon as my mother related the
affair to me, to talk to him myself, and dissuade
him from the match; but it was too late *then*, I
found, to do anything; for, unluckily, I was not
in the way at first, and knew nothing of it till
after the breach had taken place, when it was
not for me, you know, to interfere. But had I
been informed of it a few hours earlier, I think
it is most probable that something might have
been hit on. I certainly should have represented
it to Edward in a very strong light. "My dear
fellow," I should have said, " consider what you
are doing. You are making a most disgraceful
connexion, and such a one as your family are

unanimous in disapproving." I cannot help thinking, in short, that means might have been found. But now it is all too late. He must be starved, you know; that is certain; absolutely starved.'

He had just settled this point with great composure, when the entrance of Mrs. John Dashwood put an end to the subject. But though *she* never spoke of it out of her own family, Elinor could see its influence on her mind, in the something like confusion of countenance with which she entered, and an attempt at cordiality in her behaviour to herself. She even proceeded so far as to be concerned to find that Elinor and her sister were so soon to leave town, as she had hoped to see more of them; an exertion in which her husband, who attended her into the room, and hung enamoured over her accents, seemed to distinguish everything that was most affectionate and graceful.

CHAPTER XLII

ONE other short call in Harley Street, in which Elinor received her brother's congratulations, on their travelling so far towards Barton without any expense, and on Colonel Brandon's being to follow them to Cleveland in a day or two, completed the intercourse of the brother and sisters in town; and a faint invitation from Fanny, to come to Norland whenever it should happen to be in their way, which of all things was the most unlikely to occur, with a more warm, though less public assurance, from John to Elinor, of the promptitude with which he should come to see her at Delaford, was all that foretold any meeting in the country.

It amused her to observe that all her friends seemed determined to send her to Delaford; a place in which, of all others, she would now least chuse to visit or wish to reside; for not only was it considered as her future home by her brother and Mrs. Jennings, but even Lucy, when they parted, gave her a pressing invitation to visit her there.

163

Very early in April, and tolerably early in the day, the two parties from Hanover Square and Berkeley Street set out from their respective homes, to meet by appointment on the road. For the convenience of Charlotte and her child, they were to be more than two days on their journey, and Mr. Palmer, travelling more expeditiously with Colonel Brandon, was to join them at Cleveland soon after their arrival.

Marianne, few as had been her hours of comfort in London, and eager as she had long been to quit it, could not, when it came to the point, bid adieu to the house in which she had for the last time enjoyed those hopes and that confidence in Willoughby, which were now extinguished for ever, without great pain. Nor could she leave the place in which Willoughby remained busy in new engagements, and new schemes, in which *she* could have no share, without shedding many tears.

Elinor's satisfaction at the moment of removal was more positive. She had no such object for her lingering thoughts to fix on, she left no creature behind from whom it would give her a moment's regret to be divided for ever, she was pleased to be free herself from the persecution of Lucy's friendship, she was grateful for bringing her sister away unseen by Willoughby since his marriage, and she looked forward with hope to what a few months of tranquillity at Barton might do towards restoring Marianne's peace of mind, and confirming her own.

Their journey was safely performed. The second day brought them into the cherished, or the prohibited county of Somerset, for as such was it dwelt on by turns in Marianne's imagination; and in the forenoon of the third they drove up to Cleveland.

Cleveland was a spacious, modern-built house, situated on a sloping lawn. It had no park, but the pleasure-grounds were tolerably extensive; and like every other place of the same degree of importance, it had its open shrubbery, and closer wood-walk; a road of smooth gravel, winding round a plantation, led to the front; the lawn was dotted over with timber; the house itself was under the guardianship of the fir, the mountain-ash, and the acacia, and a thick screen of them altogether, interspersed with tall Lombardy poplars, shut out the offices.

Marianne entered the house with an heart swelling with emotion from the consciousness of being only eighty miles from Barton, and not thirty from Combe Magna; and before she had been five minutes within its walls, while the others were busily helping Charlotte shew her child to the housekeeper, she quitted it again, stealing away through the winding shrubberies,

now just beginning to be in beauty, to gain
a distant eminence; where, from its Grecian
temple, her eye, wandering over a wide tract
of country to the south-east, could fondly rest
on the farthest ridge of hills in the horizon, and
fancy that from their summits Combe Magna
might be seen.

In such moments of precious, of invaluable
misery, she rejoiced in tears of agony to be at
Cleveland; and as she returned by a different
circuit to the house, feeling all the happy privilege of country liberty, of wandering from place
to place in free and luxurious solitude, she resolved to spend almost every hour of every day,
while she remained with the Palmers, in the
indulgence of such solitary rambles.

She returned just in time to join the others,
as they quitted the house, on an excursion
through its more immediate premises; and the
rest of the morning was easily whiled away, in
lounging round the kitchen garden, examining
the bloom upon its walls, and listening to the
gardener's lamentations upon blights,—in dawd-
ling through the greenhouse, where the loss
of her favourite plants, unwarily exposed, and
nipped by the lingering frost, raised the laughter
of Charlotte,—and in visiting her poultry-yard,
where in the disappointed hopes of her dairy-
maid, by hens forsaking their nests, or being

stolen by a fox, or in the rapid decease of a promising young brood, she found fresh sources of merriment.

The morning was fine and dry, and Marianne, in her plan of employment abroad, had not calculated for any change of weather during their stay at Cleveland. With great surprise, therefore, did she find herself prevented by a settled rain from going out again after dinner. She had depended on a twilight walk to the Grecian temple, and perhaps all over the grounds, and an evening merely cold or damp would not have deterred her from it; but a heavy and settled rain even *she* could not fancy dry or pleasant weather for walking.

Their party was small, and the hours passed quietly away. Mrs. Palmer had her child, and Mrs. Jennings her carpet-work; they talked of the friends they had left behind, arranged Lady Middleton's engagements, and wondered whether Mr. Palmer and Colonel Brandon would get farther than Reading that night. Elinor, however little concerned in it, joined in their discourse, and Marianne, who had the knack of finding her way in every house to the library, however it might be avoided by the family in general, soon procured herself a book.

Nothing was wanting on Mrs. Palmer's side that constant and friendly good-humour could do, to make them feel themselves welcome. The openness and heartiness of her manner more than atoned for that want of recollection and elegance which made her often deficient in the forms of politeness; her kindness, recommended by so pretty a face, was engaging; her folly, though evident, was not disgusting, because it was not conceited; and Elinor could have forgiven everything but her laugh.

The two gentlemen arrived the next day to a very late dinner, affording a pleasant enlargement of the party, and a very welcome variety to their conversation, which a long morning of the same continued rain had reduced very low.

Elinor had seen so little of Mr. Palmer, and in that little had seen so much variety in his address to her sister and herself, that she knew not what to expect to find him in his own family. She found him, however, perfectly the gentleman in his behaviour to all his visitors, and only occasionally rude to his wife and her mother; she found him very capable of being a pleasant companion, and only prevented from being so always by too great an aptitude to fancy himself as much superior to people in general, as he must feel himself to be to Mrs. Jennings and Charlotte. For the rest of his character and habits, they were marked, as far as Elinor could perceive, with no traits at all unusual in his sex and time of life. He was nice in his eating, uncertain in his hours; fond of his child, though affecting to slight it; and idled away the mornings at billiards, which ought to have been devoted to business. She liked him, however, upon the whole; much better than she had expected, and in her heart was not sorry that she could like him no more; not sorry to be driven by the observation of his epicurism, his selfishness, and his conceit, to rest with complacency on the remembrance of Edward's generous temper, simple taste, and diffident feelings.

Of Edward, or at least of some of his concerns, she now received intelligence from Colonel Brandon, who had been into Dorsetshire lately; and who, treating her at once as the disinterested friend of Mr. Ferrars, and the kind confidante of himself, talked to her a great deal of the parsonage at Delaford, described its deficiencies, and told her what he meant to do himself towards removing them. His behaviour to her in this as well as in every other particular, his open pleasure in meeting her after an absence of only ten days, his readiness to converse with her, and his deference for her opinion, might very well justify Mrs. Jennings's persuasion of his attachment, and would have been enough, perhaps, had not Elinor still, as from the first, believed Marianne his real favourite, to make her suspect it herself. But as it was, such a notion had scarcely ever entered her head, except by Mrs. Jennings's suggestion; and she could not help believing herself the nicest observer of the two; she watched his eyes, while Mrs. Jennings thought only of his behaviour; and while his looks of anxious solicitude on Marianne's feeling in her head and throat the beginning of a heavy cold, because unexpressed by words, entirely escaped the latter lady's observation, *she* could discover in them the quick feelings and needless alarm of a lover.

Two delightful twilight walks on the third and fourth evenings of her being there, not merely on the dry gravel of the shrubbery, but all over the grounds, and especially in the most distant parts of them, where there was something more of wildness than in the rest, where the trees were the oldest, and the grass was the longest and wettest, had—assisted by the still greater imprudence of sitting in her wet shoes and stockings—given Marianne a cold so violent as, though for a day or two trifled with or denied, would force itself by increasing ailment on the concern of everybody, and the notice of herself. Prescriptions poured in from all quarters, and as usual were all declined. Though heavy and feverish, with a pain in her limbs, a cough, and a sore throat, a good night's rest was to cure her entirely; and it was with difficulty that Elinor prevailed on her, when she went to bed, to try one or two of the simplest of remedies.

CHAPTER XLIII

MARIANNE got up the next morning at her usual time; to every inquiry replied that she was better, and tried to prove herself so by engaging in her accustomary employments. But a day spent in sitting shivering over the fire with a book in her hand, which she was unable to read, or in lying, weary and languid, on a sofa, did not speak much in favour of her amendment; and when at last she went early to bed, more and more indisposed, Colonel Brandon was only astonished at her sister's composure, who, though attending and nursing her the whole day, against Marianne's inclination, and forcing proper medicines on her at night, trusted like Marianne to the certainty and efficacy of sleep, and felt no real alarm.

A very restless and feverish night, however, disappointed the expectation of both; and when Marianne, after persisting in rising, confessed herself unable to sit up, and returned voluntarily to her bed, Elinor was very ready to adopt Mrs.

172

Jennings's advice, of sending for the Palmers' apothecary.

He came, examined his patient, and though encouraging Miss Dashwood to expect that a very few days would restore her sister to health, yet by pronouncing her disorder to have a putrid tendency, and allowing the word 'infection' to pass his lips, gave instant alarm to Mrs. Palmer on her baby's account. Mrs. Jennings, who had been inclined from the first to think Marianne's complaint more serious than Elinor, now looked very grave on Mr. Harris's report, and confirming Charlotte's fears and caution, urged the necessity of her immediate removal with her infant; and Mr. Palmer, though treating their apprehensions as idle, found the anxiety and importunity of his wife too great to be withstood. Her departure, therefore, was fixed on; and within an hour after Mr. Harris's arrival, she set off, with her little boy and his nurse, for the house of a near relation of Mr. Palmer's, who lived a few miles on the other side of Bath; whither her husband promised, at her earnest entreaty, to join her in a day or two; and whither she was almost equally urgent with her mother to accompany her. Mrs. Jennings, however, with a kindness of heart which made Elinor really love her, declared her resolution of not stirring from Cleveland as long as Marianne remained ill, and of endeavouring, by her own attentive care, to supply to her the place of the mother she had taken her from; and Elinor found her on every occasion a most willing and active helpmate, desirous to share in all her fatigues, and often, by her better experience in nursing, of material use.

Poor Marianne, languid and low from the nature of her malady, and feeling herself universally ill, could no longer hope that to-morrow would find her recovered; and the idea of what to-morrow would have produced, but for this unlucky illness, made every ailment more severe; for on that day they were to have begun their journey home, and, attended the whole way by a servant of Mrs. Jennings, were to have taken their mother by surprise on the following forenoon. The little that she said was all in lamentation of this inevitable delay; though Elinor tried to raise her spirits, and make her believe, as she *then* really believed herself, that it would be a very short one.

The next day produced little or no alteration in the state of the patient; she certainly was not better, and except that there was no amendment, did not appear worse. Their party was now farther reduced; for Mr. Palmer, though very unwilling to go, as well from real humanity and good-nature as from a dislike of appearing to be frightened away by his wife, was persuaded at last by Colonel Brandon to perform his promise of following her; and while he was preparing to go, Colonel Brandon himself, with a much greater exertion, began to talk of going likewise. Here, however, the kindness of Mrs. Jennings interposed most acceptably; for to send the Colonel away while his love was in so much uneasiness on her sister's account, would be to deprive them both, she thought, of every comfort; and therefore, telling him at once that his stay at Cleveland was necessary to herself, that she should want him to play at piquet of an evening while Miss Dashwood was above with her sister, etc., she urged him so strongly to remain that he, who was gratifying the first wish of his own heart by a compliance, could not long even affect to demur; especially as Mrs. Jennings's entreaty was warmly seconded by Mr. Palmer, who seemed to feel a relief to himself in leaving behind him a person so well able to assist or advise Miss Dashwood in any emergence.

Marianne was of course kept in ignorance of all these arrangements. She knew not that she had been the means of sending the owners of Cleveland away, in about seven days from the time of their arrival. It gave her no surprise that she saw nothing of Mrs. Palmer! and as it gave her likewise no concern, she never mentioned her name.

Two days passed away from the time of Mr. Palmer's departure, and her situation continued, with little variation, the same. Mr. Harris, who attended her every day, still talked boldly of a speedy recovery, and Miss Dashwood was equally sanguine; but the expectation of the others was by no means so cheerful. Mrs. Jennings had determined very early in the seizure that Marianne would never get over it, and Colonel Brandon, who was chiefly of use in listening to Mrs. Jennings's forebodings, was not in a state of mind to resist their influence. He tried to reason himself out of fears which the different judgment of the apothecary seemed to render absurd; but the many hours of each day in which he was left entirely alone were but too favourable for the admission of every melancholy idea, and he could not expel from his mind the persuasion that he should see Marianne no more.

On the morning of the third day, however, the gloomy anticipations of both were almost done away; for when Mr. Harris arrived, he declared his patient materially better. Her pulse was much stronger and every symptom more favourable than on the preceding visit. Elinor, confirmed in every pleasant hope, was all cheerfulness; rejoicing that in her letters to

her mother, she had pursued her own judgment
rather than her friend's, in making very light of
the indisposition which delayed them at Cleveland, and almost fixing on the time when
Marianne would be able to travel.

But the day did not close so auspiciously as it
began. Towards the evening Marianne became
ill again, growing more heavy, restless, and
uncomfortable than before. Her sister, however, still sanguine, was willing to attribute the
change to nothing more than the fatigue of
having sat up to have her bed made; and carefully administering the cordials prescribed, saw
her with satisfaction sink at last into a slumber
from which she expected the most beneficial
effects. Her sleep, though not so quiet as
Elinor wished to see it, lasted a considerable
time; and anxious to observe the result of it
herself, she resolved to sit with her during the
whole of it. Mrs. Jennings, knowing nothing
of any change in the patient, went unusually
early to bed; her maid, who was one of the
principal nurses, was recreating herself in the
housekeeper's room, and Elinor remained alone
with Marianne.

The repose of the latter became more and
more disturbed; and her sister, who watched
with unremitting attention her continual change
of posture, and heard the frequent but inarticu-

late sounds of complaint which passed her lips,
was almost wishing to rouse her from so painful
a slumber, when Marianne, suddenly awakened
by some accidental noise in the house, started
hastily up, and, with feverish wildness, cried
out—

'Is mama coming?'

'Not yet,' replied the other, concealing her
terror, and assisting Marianne to lie down again;
'but she will be here, I hope, before it is long.
It is a great way, you know, from hence to
Barton.'

'But she must not go round by London,'
cried Marianne, in the same hurried manner.
'I shall never see her if she goes to London.'

Elinor perceived with alarm that she was not
quite herself, and while attempting to soothe her,
eagerly felt her pulse. It was lower and quicker
than ever; and Marianne still talking wildly of
mama, her alarm increased so rapidly, as to
determine her on sending instantly for Mr.
Harris, and despatching a messenger to Barton
for her mother. To consult with Colonel
Brandon on the best means of effecting the
latter, was a thought which immediately followed the resolution of its performance; and
as soon as she had rung up the maid to take her
place by her sister, she hastened down to the
drawing-room, where she knew he was generally

to be found at a much later hour than at present.

It was no time for hesitation. Her fears and her difficulties were immediately before him. Her fears, he had no courage, no confidence to attempt the removal of;—he listened to them in silent despondence;—but her difficulties were instantly obviated, for with a readiness that seemed to speak the occasion, and the service prearranged in his mind, he offered himself as the messenger who should fetch Mrs. Dashwood. Elinor made no resistance that was not easily overcome. She thanked him with a brief, though fervent gratitude, and while he went to hurry off his servant with a message to Mr. Harris, and an order for post-horses directly, she wrote a few lines to her mother.

The comfort of such a friend at that moment as Colonel Brandon—of such a companion for her mother,—how gratefully was it felt!—a companion whose judgment would guide, whose attendance must relieve, and whose friendship might soothe her!—as far as the shock of such a summons *could* be lessened to her, his presence, his manners, his assistance, would lessen it.

He, meanwhile, whatever he might feel, acted with all the firmness of a collected mind, made every necessary arrangement with the utmost despatch, and calculated with exactness the time

in which she might look for his return. Not
a moment was lost in delay of any kind. The
horses arrived, even before they were expected,
and Colonel Brandon, only pressing her hand
with a look of solemnity, and a few words
spoken too low to reach her ear, hurried into
the carriage. It was then about twelve o'clock,
and she returned to her sister's apartment to
wait for the arrival of the apothecary, and to
watch by her the rest of the night. It was
a night of almost equal suffering to both. Hour
after hour passed away in sleepless pain and
delirium on Marianne's side, and in the most
cruel anxiety on Elinor's, before Mr. Harris
appeared. Her apprehensions once raised, paid
by their excess for all her former security; and
the servant who sat up with her, for she would
not allow Mrs. Jennings to be called, only tor-
tured her more by hints of what her mistress
had always thought.

Marianne's ideas were still, at intervals, fixed
incoherently on her mother, and whenever she
mentioned her name, it gave a pang to the
heart of poor Elinor, who, reproaching herself
for having trifled with so many days of illness,
and wretched for some immediate relief, fancied
that all relief might soon be in vain, that everything had been delayed too long, and pictured
to herself her suffering mother, arriving too

late to see this darling child, or to see her
rational.

She was on the point of sending again for
Mr. Harris, or if *he* could not come, for some
other advice, when the former—but not till after
five o'clock — arrived.   His opinion, however,
made some little amends for his delay, for though
acknowledging a very unexpected and unpleasant
alteration in his patient, he would not allow the
danger to be material, and talked of the relief
which a fresh mode of treatment must procure,
with a confidence which, in a lesser degree, was
communicated to Elinor.   He promised to call
again, in the course of three or four hours, and
left both the patient and her anxious attendant
more composed than he had found them.

With strong concern, and with many re-
proaches for not being called to their aid, did
Mrs. Jennings hear in the morning of what had
passed.   Her former apprehensions, now with
greater reason restored, left her no doubt of the
event ; and though trying to speak comfort
to Elinor, her conviction of her sister's danger
would not allow her to offer the comfort of hope.
Her heart was really grieved.   The rapid decay,
the early death of a girl so young, so lovely as
Marianne, must have struck a less interested
person with concern.   On Mrs. Jennings's compassion she had other claims.   She had been for

three months her companion, was still under her care, and she was known to have been greatly injured, and long unhappy. The distress of her sister too, particularly a favourite, was before her;—and as for their mother, when Mrs. Jennings considered that Marianne might probably be to *her* what Charlotte was to herself, her sympathy in *her* sufferings was very sincere.

Mr. Harris was punctual in his second visit; but he came to be disappointed in his hopes of what the last would produce. His medicines had failed;—the fever was unabated; and Marianne, only more quiet—not more herself —remained in an heavy stupor. Elinor, catching all, and more than all, his fears in a moment, proposed to call in farther advice. But he judged it unnecessary: he had still something more to try, some fresh application, of whose success he was almost as confident as the last; and his visit concluded with encouraging assurances which reached the ear, but could not enter the heart of Miss Dashwood. She was calm, except when she thought of her mother, but she was almost hopeless; and in this state she continued till noon, scarcely stirring from her sister's bed, her thoughts wandering from one image of grief, one suffering friend to another, and her spirits oppressed to the utmost by the conversation of Mrs. Jennings, who scrupled not to attribute the severity and danger of this attack to the many weeks of previous indisposition which Marianne's disappointment had brought on. Elinor felt all the reasonableness of the idea, and it gave fresh misery to her reflections.

About noon, however, she began—but with a caution, a dread of some disappointment, which for some time kept her silent, even to her friend —to fancy, to hope she could perceive a slight amendment in her sister's pulse;—she waited, watched, examined it again and again;—and at last, with an agitation more difficult to bury under exterior calmness than all her foregoing distress, ventured to communicate her hopes. Mrs. Jennings, though forced on examination to acknowledge a temporary revival, tried to keep her young friend from indulging a thought of its continuance; and Elinor, conning over every injunction of distrust, told herself likewise not to hope. But it was too late. Hope had already entered; and feeling all its anxious flutter, she bent over her sister to watch—she hardly knew for what. Half an hour passed away, and the favourable symptom yet blessed her. Others even arose to confirm it. Her breath, her skin, her lips, all flattered Elinor with signs of amendment, and Marianne fixed her eyes on her with a rational, though languid, gaze. Anxiety and hope now oppressed her in equal degrees, and left her no moment of tranquillity till the arrival of Mr. Harris at four o'clock ;— when his assurances, his felicitations on a recovery in her sister even surpassing his expectation, gave her confidence, comfort, and tears of joy.

Marianne was in every respect materially better, and he declared her entirely out of danger. Mrs. Jennings, perhaps satisfied with the partial justification of her forebodings which had been found in their late alarm, allowed herself to trust in his judgment, and admitted with unfeigned joy, and soon with unequivocal cheerfulness, the probability of an entire recovery.

Elinor could not be cheerful. Her joy was of a different kind, and led to anything rather than to gaiety. Marianne restored to life, health, friends, and to her doating mother, was an idea to fill her heart with sensations of exquisite comfort, and expand it in fervent gratitude ; but it led to no outward demonstrations of joy, no words, no smiles. All within Elinor's breast was satisfaction, silent and strong.

She continued by the side of her sister with little intermission the whole afternoon, calming every fear, satisfying every inquiry of her enfeebled spirits, supplying every succour, and

184

watching almost every look and every breath. The possibility of a relapse would, of course, in some moments, occur to remind her of what anxiety was; but when she saw on her frequent and minute examination, that every symptom of recovery continued, and saw Marianne at six o'clock sink into a quiet, steady, and to all appearance comfortable sleep, she silenced every doubt.

The time was now drawing on when Colonel Brandon might be expected back. At ten o'clock, she trusted, or at least not much later, her mother would be relieved from the dreadful suspense in which she must now be travelling towards them. The Colonel too!—perhaps scarcely less an object of pity! Oh! how slow was the progress of time which yet kept them in ignorance!

At seven o'clock, leaving Marianne still sweetly asleep, she joined Mrs. Jennings in the drawing-room to tea. Of breakfast she had been kept by her fears, and of dinner by their sudden reverse, from eating much; and the present refreshment, therefore, with such feelings of content as she brought to it, was particularly welcome. Mrs. Jennings would have persuaded her at its conclusion to take some rest before her mother's arrival, and allow *her* to take her place by Marianne; but Elinor had no sense of fatigue, no capability of sleep at that moment about her, and she was not to be kept away from her sister an unnecessary instant. Mrs. Jennings therefore, attending her up stairs into the sick-chamber, to satisfy herself that all continued right, left her there again to her charge and her thoughts, and retired to her own room to write letters and sleep.

The night was cold and stormy. The wind roared round the house, and the rain beat against the windows; but Elinor, all happiness within, regarded it not. Marianne slept through every blast, and the travellers—they had a rich reward in store, for every present inconvenience.

The clock struck eight. Had it been ten, Elinor would have been convinced that at that moment she heard a carriage driving up to the house; and so strong was the persuasion that she *did*, in spite of the *almost* impossibility of their being already come, that she moved into the adjoining dressing-closet and opened a window-shutter, to be satisfied of the truth. She instantly saw that her ears had not deceived her. The flaring lamps of a carriage were immediately in view. By their uncertain light she thought she could discern it to be drawn by four horses; and this, while it told the excess of her poor mother's alarm, gave some explanation to such unexpected rapidity.

SENSE AND SENSIBILITY

Never in her life had Elinor found it so difficult to be calm, as at that moment. The knowledge of what her mother must be feeling as the carriage stopped at the door, of her doubt—her dread—perhaps her despair!—and of what *she* had to tell!—with such knowledge it was impossible to be calm. All that remained to be done was to be speedy ; and therefore, staying only till she could leave Mrs. Jennings's maid with her sister, she hurried down stairs.

The bustle in the vestibule, as she passed along an inner lobby, assured her that they were already in the house. She rushed forwards towards the drawing-room—she entered it—and saw only Willoughby.

CHAPTER XLIV

ELINOR, starting back with a look of horror at the sight of him, obeyed the first impulse of her heart in turning instantly to quit the room, and her hand was already on the lock, when its action was suspended by his hastily advancing, and saying, in a voice rather of command than supplication—

'Miss Dashwood, for half an hour—for ten minutes—I entreat you to stay.'

'No, sir,' she replied with firmness, 'I shall *not* stay. Your business cannot be with *me*. The servants, I suppose, forgot to tell you that Mr. Palmer was not in the house.'

'Had they told me,' he cried with vehemence, 'that Mr. Palmer and all his relations were at the devil, it would not have turned me from the door. My business is with you, and only you.'

'With me!'—in the utmost amazement—'well, sir—be quick—and, if you can—less violent.'

'Sit down, and I will be both.'

188

SENSE AND SENSIBILITY

She hesitated; she knew not what to do. The possibility of Colonel Brandon's arriving and finding him there came across her. But she had promised to hear him, and her curiosity no less than her honour was engaged. After a moment's recollection, therefore, concluding that prudence required despatch, and that her acquiescence would best promote it, she walked silently towards the table and sat down. He took the opposite chair, and for half a minute not a word was said by either.

'Pray be quick, sir,' said Elinor impatiently; 'I have no time to spare.'

He was sitting in an attitude of deep meditation, and seemed not to hear her.

'Your sister,' said he, with abruptness, a moment afterwards, 'is out of danger. I heard it from the servant. God be praised! But is it true?—is it really true?'

Elinor would not speak. He repeated the inquiry with yet greater eagerness.

'For God's sake tell me, is she out of danger, or is she not?'

'We hope she is.'

He rose up, and walked across the room.

'Had I known as much half an hour ago— But since I *am* here'—speaking with a forced vivacity as he returned to his seat—'what does it signify? For once, Miss Dashwood—it will be the last time, perhaps—let us be cheerful together.—I am in a fine mood for gaiety. Tell me honestly'—a deeper glow overspreading his cheeks—'do you think me most a knave or a fool?'

Elinor looked at him with greater astonishment than ever. She began to think that he must be in liquor; the strangeness of such a visit, and of such manners, seemed no otherwise intelligible; and with this impression she immediately rose, saying—

'Mr. Willoughby, I advise you at present to return to Combe. I am not at leisure to remain with you longer. Whatever your business may be with me, it will be better recollected and explained to-morrow.'

'I understand you,' he replied, with an expressive smile, and a voice perfectly calm. 'Yes, I am very drunk. A pint of porter with my cold beef at Marlborough was enough to overset me.'

'At Marlborough!' cried Elinor, more and more at a loss to understand what he would be at.

'Yes—I left London this morning at eight o'clock, and the only ten minutes I have spent out of my chaise since that time procured me a nuncheon at Marlborough.'

The steadiness of his manner, and the intelligence of his eye as he spoke, convincing Elinor, that whatever other unpardonable folly might bring him to Cleveland, he was not brought there by intoxication, she said, after a moment's recollection—

'Mr. Willoughby, you *ought* to feel, and I certainly *do*—that after what has passed—your coming here in this manner, and forcing yourself upon my notice, requires a very particular excuse. What is it that you mean by it?'

'I mean,' said he, with serious energy, 'if I can, to make you hate me one degree less than you do *now*. I mean to offer some kind of explanation, some kind of apology, for the past —to open my whole heart to you, and by convincing you, that though I have been always a blockhead, I have not been always a rascal, to obtain something like forgiveness from Ma— from your sister.'

'Is this the real reason of your coming?'

'Upon my soul it is,' was his answer, with a warmth which brought all the former Willoughby to her remembrance, and in spite of herself made her think him sincere.

'If that is all, you may be satisfied already, for Marianne *does*—she has *long* forgiven you.'

'Has she!' he cried, in the same eager tone. 'Then she has forgiven me before she ought

191

to have done it. But she shall forgive me again, and on more reasonable grounds. *Now*, will you listen to me?'

Elinor bowed her assent.

'I do not know,' said he, after a pause of expectation on her side, and thoughtfulness on his own, 'how *you* may have accounted for my behaviour to your sister, or what diabolical motive you may have imputed to me. Perhaps you will hardly think the better of me,—it is worth the trial, however, and you shall hear everything. When I first became intimate in your family, I had no other intention, no other view in the acquaintance than to pass my time pleasantly while I was obliged to remain in Devonshire, more pleasantly than I had ever done before. Your sister's lovely person and interesting manners could not but please me; and her behaviour to me, almost from the first, was of a kind—— It is astonishing, when I reflect on what I was, and what *she* was, that my heart should have been so insensible!—But at first, I must confess, my vanity only was elevated by it. Careless of her happiness, thinking only of my own amusement, giving way to feelings which I had always been too much in the habit of indulging, I endeavoured, by every means in my power, to make myself pleasing to her, without any design of returning her affection.'

Miss Dashwood at this point, turning her eyes on him with the most angry contempt, stopped him, by saying—

'It is hardly worth while, Mr. Willoughby, for you to relate, or for me to listen any longer. Such a beginning as this cannot be followed by anything. Do not let me be pained by hearing anything more on the subject.'

'I insist on your hearing the whole of it,' he replied. 'My fortune was never large, and I had always been expensive, always in the habit of associating with people of better income than myself. Every year since my coming of age, or even before, I believe, had added to my debts; and though the death of my old cousin, Mrs. Smith, was to set me free, yet that event being uncertain, and possibly far distant, it had been for some time my intention to re-establish my circumstances by marrying a woman of fortune. To attach myself to your sister, therefore, was not a thing to be thought of;—and with a meanness, selfishness, cruelty—which no indignant, no contemptuous look, even of yours, Miss Dashwood, can ever reprobate too much —I was acting in this manner, trying to engage her regard, without a thought of returning it. But one thing may be said for me, even in that horrid state of selfish vanity, I did not know the extent of the injury I meditated, because

I did not *then* know what it was to love. But
have I ever known it?—Well may it be doubted;
for, had I really loved, could I have sacrificed
my feelings to vanity, to avarice?—or, what is
more, could I have sacrificed hers?—But I have
done it. To avoid a comparative poverty, which
her affection and her society would have deprived of all its horrors, I have, by raising
myself to affluence, lost everything that could
make it a blessing.'

'You did, then,' said Elinor, a little softened,
'believe yourself at one time attached to her.'

'To have resisted such attractions, to have
withstood such tenderness! Is there a man on
earth who could have done it? Yes, I found
myself, by insensible degrees, sincerely fond of
her; and the happiest hours of my life were
what I spent with her, when I felt my intentions
were strictly honourable, and my feelings blame-
less. Even *then*, however, when fully determined
on paying my addresses to her, I allowed myself
most improperly to put off, from day to day,
the moment of doing it, from an unwillingness
to enter into an engagement while my circumstances were so greatly embarrassed. I will not
reason here—nor will I stop for *you* to expatiate
on the absurdity, and the worse than absurdity,
of scrupling to engage my faith where my honour
was already bound. The event has proved that

I was a cunning fool, providing with great cir-
cumspection for a possible opportunity of making
myself contemptible and wretched for ever. At
last, however, my resolution was taken, and I
had determined, as soon as I could engage her
alone, to justify the attentions I had so invariably
paid her, and openly assure her of an affection
which I had already taken such pains to display.
But in the interim—in the interim of the very
few hours that were to pass, before I could have
an opportunity of speaking with her in private
—a circumstance occurred—an unlucky circumstance, to ruin all my resolution, and with it all
my comfort. A discovery took place '—here he
hesitated and looked down. 'Mrs. Smith had
somehow or other been informed, I imagine by
some distant relation, whose interest it was to
deprive me of her favour, of an affair, a connexion
—but I need not explain myself farther,' he
added, looking at her with a heightened colour
and an inquiring eye, 'your particular intimacy
—you have probably heard the whole story
long ago.'

'I have,' returned Elinor, colouring likewise,
and hardening her heart anew against any compassion for him, 'I have heard it all. And how
you will explain away any part of your guilt in
that dreadful business, I confess is beyond my
comprehension.'

'Remember,' cried Willoughby, 'from whom you received the account. Could it be an impartial one? I acknowledge that her situation and her character ought to have been respected by me. I do not mean to justify myself, but at the same time cannot leave you to suppose that I have nothing to urge—that because she was injured, she was irreproachable; and because *I* was a libertine, *she* must be a saint. If the violence of her passions, the weakness of her understanding — I do not mean, however, to defend myself. Her affection for me deserved better treatment, and I often, with great self-reproach, recall the tenderness which, for a very short time, had the power of creating any return. I wish—I heartily wish it had never been. But I have injured more than herself; and I have injured one whose affection for me (may I say it?) was scarcely less warm than hers, and whose mind—oh! how infinitely superior!'

'Your indifference, however, towards that unfortunate girl—I must say it, unpleasant to me as the discussion of such a subject may well be—your indifference is no apology for your cruel neglect of her. Do not think yourself excused by any weakness, any natural defect of understanding on her side, in the wanton cruelty so evident on yours. You must have known, that while you were enjoying yourself in Devonshire, pursuing fresh schemes, always gay, always happy, she was reduced to the extremest indigence.'

'But, upon my soul, I did *not* know it,' he warmly replied ; 'I did not recollect that I had omitted to give her my direction ; and common-sense might have told her how to find it out.'

'Well, sir, and what said Mrs. Smith ?'

'She taxed me with the offence at once, and my confusion may be guessed. The purity of her life, the formality of her notions, her ignorance of the world—everything was against me. The matter itself I could not deny, and vain was every endeavour to soften it. She was previously disposed, I believe, to doubt the morality of my conduct in general, and was moreover discontented with the very little attention, the very little portion of my time that I had bestowed on her, in my present visit. In short, it ended in a total breach. By one measure I might have saved myself. In the height of her morality, good woman! she offered to forgive the past if I would marry Eliza. That could not be—and I was formally dismissed from her favour and her house. The night following this affair—I was to go the next morning—was spent by me in deliberating on what my future conduct should be. The struggle was great—but it ended too soon. My affection for Marianne, my thorough conviction of her attachment to me—it was all insufficient to outweigh that dread of poverty, or get the better of those false ideas of the necessity of riches, which I was naturally inclined to feel, and expensive society had increased. I had reason to believe myself secure of my present wife, if I chose to address her, and I persuaded myself to think that nothing else in common prudence remained for me to do. An heavy scene, however, awaited me, before I could leave Devonshire : I was engaged to dine with you on that very day ; some apology was therefore necessary for my breaking the engagement. But whether I should write this apology, or deliver it in person, was a point of long debate. To see Marianne I felt would be dreadful, and I even doubted whether I could see her again, and keep to my resolution. In that point, however, I undervalued my own magnanimity, as the event declared ; for I went, I saw her, and saw her miserable, and left her miserable —and left her, hoping never to see her again.'

'Why did you call, Mr. Willoughby ?' said Elinor reproachfully ; 'a note would have answered every purpose. Why was it necessary to call ?'

'It was necessary to my own pride. I could not bear to leave the country in a manner that might lead you, or the rest of the neighbour-

hood, to suspect any part of what had really
passed between Mrs. Smith and myself, and I
resolved therefore on calling at the cottage, in
my way to Honiton. The sight of your dear
sister, however, was really dreadful; and to
heighten the matter, I found her alone. You
were all gone, I do not know where. I had left
her only the evening before, so fully, so firmly
resolved within myself on doing right! A few
hours were to have engaged her to me for ever;
and I remember how happy, how gay were my
spirits, as I walked from the cottage to Allenham, satisfied with myself, delighted with everybody! But in this, our last interview of
friendship, I approached her with a sense of
guilt that almost took from me the power of
dissembling. Her sorrow, her disappointment,
her deep regret, when I told her that I was
obliged to leave Devonshire so immediately—I
never shall forget it; united, too, with such
reliance, such confidence in me! O God! what
an hard-hearted rascal I was!'

They were both silent for a few moments.
Elinor first spoke.

'Did you tell her that you should soon return?'

'I do not know what I told her,' he replied
impatiently; 'less than was due to the past,
beyond a doubt, and in all likelihood much
more than was justified by the future. I cannot

think of it—it won't do. Then came your dear mother to torture me farther, with all her kindness and confidence. Thank Heaven! it *did* torture me. I was miserable. Miss Dashwood, you cannot have an idea of the comfort it gives me to look back on my own misery. I owe such a grudge to myself for the stupid, rascally folly of my own heart, that all my past sufferings under it are only triumph and exultation to me now. Well, I went, left all that I loved, and went to those to whom, at best, I was only indifferent. My journey to town—travelling with my own horses, and therefore so tediously —no creature to speak to—my own reflections so cheerful—when I looked forward everything so inviting!—when I looked back at Barton, the picture so soothing!—oh! it was a blessed journey.'

He stopped.

'Well, sir,' said Elinor, who, though pitying him, grew impatient for his departure, ' and this is all ? '

'All!—no—have you forgot what passed in town? That infamous letter! Did she shew it you?'

'Yes, I saw every note that passed.'

'When the first of hers reached me (as it immediately did, for I was in town the whole time), what I felt is, in the common phrase,

not to be expressed ; in a more simple one—
perhaps too simple to raise any emotion—my
feelings were very, very painful. Every line,
every word, was—in the hackneyed metaphor
which their dear writer, were she here, would
forbid—a dagger to my heart. To know that
Marianne was in town was, in the same language,
a thunderbolt. Thunderbolts and daggers !—
what a reproof would she have given me ! Her
taste, her opinions—I believe they are better
known to me than my own, and I am sure they
are dearer.'

Elinor's heart, which had undergone many
changes in the course of this extraordinary conversation, was now softened again ; yet she felt
it her duty to check such ideas in her companion
as the last.

'This is not right, Mr. Willoughby. Remember that you are married. Relate only
what in your conscience you think necessary for
me to hear.'

'Marianne's note, by assuring me that I was
still as dear to her as in former days—that, in
spite of the many, many weeks we had been
separated, she was as constant in her own feelings, and as full of faith in the constancy of
mine, as ever, awakened all my remorse. I say
awakened, because time and London, business
and dissipation, had, in some measure, quieted

it, and I had been growing a fine hardened
villain, fancying myself indifferent to her, and
chusing to fancy that she too must have become
indifferent to me ; talking to myself of our past
attachment as a mere idle, trifling business,
shrugging up my shoulders in proof of its being
so, and silencing every reproach, overcoming
every scruple, by secretly saying now and then,
" I shall be heartily glad to hear she is well
married." But this note made me know myself
better. I felt that she was infinitely dearer to
me than any other woman in the world, and that
I was using her infamously. But everything
was then just settled between Miss Grey and
me. To retreat was impossible. All that I had
to do was to avoid you both. I sent no answer
to Marianne, intending by that means to preserve myself from her farther notice ; and for
some time I was even determined not to call in
Berkeley Street ; but at last, judging it wiser to
affect the air of a cool, common acquaintance
than anything else, I watched you all safely out
of the house one morning, and left my name.'

' Watched us out of the house ! '

' Even so. You would be surprised to hear
how often I watched you, how often I was on
the point of falling in with you. I have entered
many a shop to avoid your sight as the carriage
drove by. Lodging as I did in Bond Street,

there was hardly a day in which I did not catch
a glimpse of one or other of you; and nothing
but the most constant watchfulness on my side,
a most invariably prevailing desire to keep out
of your sight, could have separated us so long.
I avoided the Middletons as much as possible,
as well as everybody else who was likely to
prove an acquaintance in common. Not aware
of their being in town, however, I blundered on
Sir John, I believe, the first day of his coming,
and the day after I called at Mrs. Jennings's.
He asked me to a party, a dance at his house in
the evening. Had he *not* told me, as an inducement, that you and your sister were to be there,
I should have felt it too certain a thing to trust
myself near him. The next morning brought
another short note from Marianne—still affectionate, open, artless, confiding—everything that
could make *my* conduct most hateful. I could
not answer it. I tried, but could not frame a
sentence. But I thought of her, I believe,
every moment of the day. If *you* can pity me,
Miss Dashwood, pity my situation as it was
then. With my head and heart full of your
sister, I was forced to play the happy lover to
another woman! Those three or four weeks
were worse than all. Well, at last, as I need
not tell you, you were forced on me: and what
a sweet figure I cut! what an evening of agony

it was! Marianne, beautiful as an angel, on one side, calling me Willoughby in such a tone! O God!—holding out her hand to me, asking me for an explanation with those bewitching eyes fixed in such speaking solicitude on my face! and Sophia, jealous as the devil, on the other hand, looking all that was—— Well, it does not signify; it is over now. Such an evening! I ran away from you all as soon as I could, but not before I had seen Marianne's sweet face as white as death. *That* was the last, last look I ever had of her—the last manner in which she appeared to me. It was an horrid sight! Yet when I thought of her to-day as really dying, it was a kind of comfort to me to imagine that I knew exactly how she would appear to those who saw her last in this world. She was before me, constantly before me, as I travelled, in the same look and hue.'

A short pause of mutual thoughtfulness succeeded. Willoughby, first rousing himself, broke it thus—

'Well, let me make haste and be gone. Your sister is certainly better, certainly out of danger?'

'We are assured of it.'

'Your poor mother too! doating on Marianne!'

'But the letter, Mr. Willoughby, your own letter; have you anything to say about that?'

204

'Yes, yes, *that* in particular. Your sister wrote to me again, you know, the very next morning. You saw what she said. I was breakfasting at the Ellisons'; and her letter, with some others, was brought to me there from my lodgings. It happened to catch Sophia's eye before it caught mine; and its size, the elegance of the paper, the handwriting, altogether immediately gave her a suspicion. Some vague report had reached her before of my attachment to some young lady in Devonshire, and what had passed within her observation the preceding evening had marked who the young lady was, and made her more jealous than ever. Affecting that air of playfulness, therefore, which is delightful in a woman one loves, she opened the letter directly, and read its contents. She was well paid for her impudence. She read what made her wretched. Her wretchedness I could have borne, but her passion—her malice—at all events it must be appeased. And in short, what do you think of my wife's style of letter-writing? —delicate, tender, truly feminine was it not?'

'Your wife!—the letter was in your own handwriting.'

'Yes, but I had only the credit of servilely copying such sentences as I was ashamed to put my name to. The original was all her own, her own happy thoughts and gentle diction. But

what could I do?—we were engaged, everything
in preparation, the day almost fixed—but I am
talking like a fool. Preparation!—day!—In
honest words, her money was necessary to me,
and in a situation like mine anything was to be
done to prevent a rupture. And after all, what
did it signify to my character, in the opinion of
Marianne and her friends, in what language my
answer was couched? It must have been only
to one end. My business was to declare myself
a scoundrel, and whether I did it with a bow or
a bluster was of little importance. " I am ruined
for ever in their opinion," said I to myself; " I
am shut out for ever from their society; they
already think me an unprincipled fellow, this
letter will only make them think me a black-
guard one." Such were my reasonings as, in a
sort of desperate carelessness, I copied my wife's
words, and parted with the last relics of Marianne. Her three notes—unluckily they were
all in my pocket-book, or I should have denied
their existence, and hoarded them for ever; I
was forced to put them up, and could not even
kiss them. And the lock of hair—that too I
had always carried about me in the same pocket-
book, which was now searched by madam with
the most ingratiating virulence—the dear lock
—all, every memento was torn from me.'

'You are very wrong, Mr. Willoughby, very

blamable,' said Elinor, while her voice, in spite of herself, betrayed her compassionate emotion; 'you ought not to speak in this way, either of Mrs. Willoughby or my sister. You have made your own choice. It was not forced on you. Your wife has a claim to your politeness, to your respect, at least. She must be attached to you, or she would not have married you. To treat her with unkindness, to speak of her slightingly, is no atonement to Marianne, nor can I suppose it a relief to your own conscience.'

'Do not talk to me of my wife,' said he, with a heavy sigh. 'She does not deserve your compassion. She knew I had no regard for her when we married. Well, married we were, and came down to Combe Magna to be happy, and afterwards returned to town to be gay. And now do you pity me, Miss Dashwood? or have I said all this to no purpose? Am I—be it only one degree—am I less guilty in your opinion than I was before? My intentions were not always wrong. Have I explained away any part of my guilt?'

'Yes, you have certainly removed something —a little. You have proved yourself, on the whole, less faulty than I had believed you. You have proved your heart less wicked, much less wicked. But I hardly know—the misery that you have inflicted—I hardly know what could have made it worse.'

'Will you repeat to your sister, when she is recovered, what I have been telling you? Let me be a little lightened too in her opinion as well as in yours. You tell me that she has forgiven me already. Let me be able to fancy that a better knowledge of my heart, and of my present feelings, will draw from her a more spontaneous, more natural, more gentle, less dignified forgiveness. Tell her of my misery and my penitence, tell her that my heart was never inconstant to her, and if you will, that at this moment she is dearer to me than ever.'

'I will tell her all that is necessary to what may comparatively be called your justification. But you have not explained to me the particular reason of your coming now, nor how you heard of her illness.'

'Last night, in Drury Lane lobby, I ran against Sir John Middleton, and when he saw who I was—for the first time these two months —he spoke to me. That he had cut me ever since my marriage, I had seen without surprise or resentment. Now, however, his good-natured, honest, stupid soul, full of indignation against me, and concern for your sister, could not resist the temptation of telling me what he knew ought to, though probably he did not think it *would*, vex me horribly. As bluntly as he could speak it, therefore, he told me that Marianne Dashwood was dying of a putrid fever at Cleveland—a letter that morning received from Mrs. Jennings declared her danger most imminent—the Palmers all gone off in a fright, etc. I was too much shocked to be able to pass myself off as insensible, even to the undiscerning Sir John. His heart was softened in seeing mine suffer; and so much of his ill-will was done away, that when we parted, he almost shook me by the hand, while he reminded me of an old promise about a pointer puppy. What I felt on hearing that your sister was dying— and dying, too, believing me the greatest villain upon earth, scorning, hating me in her latest moments—for how could I tell what horrid projects might not have been imputed?—*One* person I was sure would represent me as capable of anything. What I felt was dreadful! My resolution was soon made, and at eight o'clock this morning I was in my carriage. Now you know all.'

Elinor made no answer. Her thoughts were silently fixed on the irreparable injury which too early an independence and its consequent habits of idleness, dissipation, and luxury, had made in the mind, the character, the happiness, of a man who, to every advantage of person and talents, united a disposition naturally open and honest, and a feeling, affectionate temper. The world had made him extravagant and vain; extravagance and vanity had made him cold-hearted and selfish. Vanity, while seeking its own guilty triumph at the expense of another, had involved him in a real attachment, which extravagance, or at least its offspring necessity, had required to be sacrificed. Each faulty propensity, in leading him to evil, had led him likewise to punishment. The attachment from which against honour, against feeling, against every better interest he had outwardly torn himself, now, when no longer allowable, governed every thought; and the connexion, for the sake of which he had, with little scruple, left her sister to misery, was likely to prove a source of unhappiness to himself of a far more incurable nature. From a reverie of this kind she was recalled at the end of some minutes by Willoughby, who, rousing himself from a reverie at least equally painful, started up in preparation for going, and said—

'There is no use in staying here; I must be off.'

'Are you going back to town?'

'No; to Combe Magna. I have business there; from thence to town in a day or two. Good-bye.'

He held out his hand. She could not refuse to give him hers ; he pressed it with affection.

'And you *do* think something better of me than you did?' said he, letting it fall, and leaning against the mantelpiece, as if forgetting he was to go.

Elinor assured him that she did ; that she forgave, pitied him, wished him well—was even interested in his happiness — and added some gentle counsel as to the behaviour most likely to promote it. His answer was not very encouraging.

'As to that,' said he, 'I must rub through the world as well as I can. Domestic happiness is out of the question. If, however, I am allowed to think that you and yours feel an interest in my fate and actions, it may be the means—it may put me on my guard—at least, it may be something to live for. Marianne, to be sure, is lost to me for ever. Were I even, by any blessed chance, at liberty again——'

Elinor stopped him with a reproof.

'Well,' he replied, 'once more good-bye. I shall now go away and live in dread of one event.'

'What do you mean ?'

'Your sister's marriage.'

'You are very wrong. She can never be more lost to you than she is now.'

'But she will be gained by some one else.

211

And if that some one should be the very he whom, of all others, I could least bear—— But I will not stay to rob myself of all your compassionate goodwill, by shewing that where I have most injured I can least forgive. Goodbye; God bless you!'

And with these words, he almost ran out of the room.

CHAPTER XLV

ELINOR, for some time after he left her, for some time even after the sound of his carriage had died away, remained too much oppressed by a crowd of ideas, widely differing in themselves, but of which sadness was the general result, to think even of her sister.

Willoughby—he whom only half an hour ago she had abhorred as the most worthless of men —Willoughby, in spite of all his faults, excited a degree of commiseration for the sufferings produced by them, which made her think of him as now separated for ever from her family with a tenderness, a regret, rather in proportion, as she soon acknowledged within herself, to his wishes than to his merits. She felt that his influence over her mind was heightened by circumstances which ought not in reason to have weight; by that person of uncommon attraction—that open, affectionate, and lively manner which it was no merit to possess; and by that still ardent love for Marianne, which it was not even innocent to indulge. But she felt that it was so, long, long before she could feel his influence less.

When at last she returned to the unconscious Marianne, she found her just awaking, refreshed by so long and sweet a sleep to the extent of her hopes. Elinor's heart was full. The past, the present, the future — Willoughby's visit, Marianne's safety, and her mother's expected arrival, threw her altogether into an agitation of spirits which kept off every indication of fatigue, and made her only fearful of betraying herself to her sister. Short was the time, however, in which that fear could affect her, for within half an hour after Willoughby's leaving the house, she was again called downstairs by the sound of another carriage. Eager to save her mother from every unnecessary moment's horrible suspense, she ran immediately into the hall, and reached the outward door just in time to receive and support her as she entered it.

Mrs. Dashwood, whose terror as they drew near the house had produced almost the conviction of Marianne's being no more, had no voice to inquire after her, no voice even for Elinor; but *she*, waiting neither for salutation nor inquiry, instantly gave the joyful relief;— and her mother, catching it with all her usual warmth, was in a moment as much overcome by her happiness as she had been before by her fears. She was supported into the drawing-room between her daughter and her friend: and there, shedding tears of joy, though still unable to speak, embraced Elinor again and again, turning from her at intervals to press Colonel Brandon's hand, with a look which spoke at once her gratitude, and her conviction of his sharing with herself in the bliss of the moment. He shared it, however, in a silence even greater than her own.

As soon as Mrs. Dashwood had recovered herself, to see Marianne was her first desire; and in two minutes she was with her beloved child, rendered dearer to her than ever by absence, unhappiness, and danger. Elinor's delight as she saw what each felt in the meeting, was only checked by an apprehension of its robbing Marianne of farther sleep: but Mrs. Dashwood could be calm, could be even prudent, when the life of a child was at stake; and Marianne, satisfied in knowing her mother was near her, and conscious of being too weak for conversation, submitted readily to the silence and quiet prescribed by every nurse around her. Mrs. Dashwood *would* sit up with her all night, and Elinor, in compliance with her mother's entreaty, went to bed. But the rest, which one night entirely sleepless and many hours of the most wearing anxiety seemed to make requisite, was kept off by irritation of spirits. Willoughby, 'poor Willoughby,' as she now allowed herself to call him, was constantly in her thoughts; she would not but have heard his vindication for the world, and now blamed, now acquitted herself, for having judged him so harshly before. But her promise of relating it to her sister was invariably painful. She dreaded the performance of it, dreaded what its effect on Marianne might be; doubted whether, after such an explanation, she could ever be happy with another, and for a moment wished Willoughby a widower; then remembering Colonel Brandon, reproved herself, felt that to *his* sufferings and *his* constancy, far more than to his rival's, the reward of her sister was due, and wished anything rather than Mrs. Willoughby's death.

The shock of Colonel Brandon's errand at Barton had been much softened to Mrs. Dashwood by her own previous alarm; for so great was her uneasiness about Marianne, that she had already determined to set out for Cleveland on that very day, without waiting for any farther intelligence, and had so far settled her journey before his arrival, that the Careys were then expected every moment to fetch Margaret away, as her mother was unwilling to take her where there might be infection.

Marianne continued to mend every day, and

the brilliant cheerfulness of Mrs. Dashwood's looks and spirits proved her to be, as she repeatedly declared herself, one of the happiest women in the world. Elinor could not hear the declaration, nor witness its proofs, without sometimes wondering whether her mother ever recollected Edward. But Mrs. Dashwood, trusting to the temperate account of her own disappointment which Elinor had sent her, was led away by the exuberance of her joy to think only of what would increase it. Marianne was restored to her from a danger in which, as she now began to feel, her own mistaken judgment in encouraging the unfortunate attachment to Willoughby had contributed to place her; and in her recovery she had yet another source of joy, unthought of by Elinor. It was thus imparted to her, as soon as any opportunity of private conference between them occurred.

'At last we are alone. My Elinor, you do not yet know all my happiness. Colonel Brandon loves Marianne; he has told me so himself.'

Her daughter, feeling by turns both pleased and pained, surprised and not surprised, was all silent attention.

'You are never like me, dear Elinor, or I should wonder at your composure now. Had I sat down to wish for any possible good to my family, I should have fixed on Colonel Brandon's marrying one of you as the object most desirable. And I believe Marianne will be the most happy with him of the two.'

Elinor was half inclined to ask her reason for thinking so, because satisfied that none founded on an impartial consideration of their age, characters, or feelings, could be given; but her mother must always be carried away by her imagination on any interesting subject, and therefore, instead of an inquiry, she passed it off with a smile.

'He opened his whole heart to me yesterday as we travelled. It came out quite unawares, quite undesignedly. I, you may well believe, could talk of nothing but my child;—he could not conceal his distress; I saw that it equalled my own, and he, perhaps thinking that mere friendship, as the world now goes, would not justify so warm a sympathy—or rather not thinking at all, I suppose—giving way to irresistible feelings, made me acquainted with his earnest, tender, constant affection for Marianne. He has loved her, my Elinor, ever since the first moment of seeing her.'

Here, however, Elinor perceived, not the language, not the professions of Colonel Brandon, but the natural embellishments of her mother's active fancy, which fashioned everything delightful to her as it chose.

'His regard for her, infinitely surpassing anything that Willoughby ever felt or feigned, as
much more warm, as more sincere or constant—
whichever we are to call it—has subsisted
through all the knowledge of dear Marianne's
unhappy prepossession for that worthless young
man!—and without selfishness—without encouraging a hope!—could he have seen her
happy with another? Such a noble mind!—
such openness, such sincerity!—no one can be
deceived in *him*.'

'Colonel Brandon's character,' said Elinor 'as
an excellent man, is well established.'

'I know it is,' replied her mother seriously,
'or after such a warning, *I* should be the last to
encourage such affection, or even to be pleased
by it. But his coming for me as he did, with
such active, such ready friendship, is enough to
prove him one of the worthiest of men.'

'His character, however,' answered Elinor,
'does not rest on *one* act of kindness, to which
his affection for Marianne, were humanity out of
the case, would have prompted him. To Mrs.
Jennings, to the Middletons, he has been long
and intimately known; they equally love and
respect him; and even my knowledge of him,
though lately acquired, is very considerable; and
so highly do *I* value and esteem him, that if
Marianne can be happy with him, I shall be as

ready as yourself to think our connexion the greatest blessing to us in the world. What answer did you give him? Did you allow him to hope?'

'Oh! my love, I could not then talk of hope to him or to myself. Marianne might at that moment be dying. But he did not ask for hope or encouragement. His was an involuntary confidence, an irrepressible effusion to a soothing friend—not an application to a parent. Yet after a time I *did* say, for at first I was quite overcome, that if she lived, as I trusted she might, my greatest happiness would lie in promoting their marriage; and since our arrival, since our delightful security, I have repeated it to him more fully, have given him every encouragement in my power. Time, a very little time, I tell him, will do everything;—Marianne's heart is not to be wasted for ever on such a man as Willoughby. His own merits must soon secure it.'

'To judge from the Colonel's spirits, however, you have not yet made him equally sanguine.'

'No. He thinks Marianne's affection too deeply rooted for any change in it under a great length of time; and even supposing her heart again free, is too diffident of himself to believe, that with such a difference of age and disposition, he could ever attach her. There, however, he is quite mistaken. His age is only so much beyond hers as to be an advantage, as to make his character and principles fixed; and his disposition, I am well convinced, is exactly the very one to make your sister happy. And his person, his manners too, are all in his favour. My partiality does not blind me: he certainly is not so handsome as Willoughby; but, at the same time, there is something much more pleasing in his countenance. There was always a something, if you remember, in Willoughby's eyes at times, which I did not like.'

Elinor could *not* remember it; but her mother, without waiting for her assent, continued—

'And his manners, the Colonel's manners, are not only more pleasing to me than Willoughby's ever were, but they are of a kind I well know to be more solidly attaching to Marianne. Their gentleness, their genuine attention to other people, and their manly, unstudied simplicity, is much more accordant with her real disposition than the liveliness, often artificial, and often ill-timed, of the other. I am very sure myself that had Willoughby turned out as really amiable as he has proved himself the contrary, Marianne would yet never have been so happy with *him* as she will be with Colonel Brandon.'

She paused. Her daughter could not quite agree with her, but her dissent was not heard, and therefore gave no offence.

221

'At Delaford she will be within an easy distance of me,' added Mrs. Dashwood, 'even if I remain at Barton; and in all probability, for I hear it is a large village—indeed, there certainly *must* be some small house or cottage close by that would suit us quite as well as our present situation.'

Poor Elinor! here was a new scheme for getting her to Delaford! but her spirit was stubborn.

'His fortune too! for at my time of life, you know, everybody cares about *that*; and though I neither know, nor desire to know, what it really is, I am sure it must be a good one.'

Here they were interrupted by the entrance of a third person, and Elinor withdrew to think it all over in private, to wish success to her friend, and yet, in wishing it, to feel a pang for Willoughby.

CHAPTER XLVI

MARIANNE's illness, though weakening in its kind, had not been long enough to make her recovery slow ; and with youth, natural strength, and her mother's presence in aid, it proceeded so smoothly as to enable her to remove, within four days after the arrival of the latter, into Mrs. Palmer's dressing-room. When there, at her own particular request, for she was impatient to pour forth her thanks to him for fetching her mother, Colonel Brandon was invited to visit her.

His emotion in entering the room, in seeing her altered looks, and in receiving the pale hand which she immediately held out to him, was such as, in Elinor's conjecture, must arise from something more than his affection for Marianne, or the consciousness of its being known to others ; and she soon discovered in his melancholy eye and varying complexion, as he looked at her sister, the probable recurrence of many past scenes of misery to his mind, brought back by that resemblance between Marianne and

223

Eliza, already acknowledged, and now strengthened by the hollow eye, the sickly skin, the
posture of reclining weakness, and the warm
acknowledgment of peculiar obligation.

Mrs. Dashwood, not less watchful of what
passed than her daughter, but with a mind very
differently influenced, and therefore watching to
very different effect, saw nothing in the Colonel's
behaviour but what arose from the most simple
and self-evident sensations, while in the actions
and words of Marianne she persuaded herself to
think that something more than gratitude already
dawned.

At the end of another day or two, Marianne
growing visibly stronger every twelve hours,
Mrs. Dashwood, urged equally by her own and
her daughter's wishes, began to talk of removing
to Barton. On *her* measures depended those of
her two friends : Mrs. Jennings could not quit
Cleveland during the Dashwoods' stay, and
Colonel Brandon was soon brought, by their
united request, to consider his own abode there
as equally determinate, if not equally indispensable. At his and Mrs. Jennings's united request
in return, Mrs. Dashwood was prevailed on to
accept the use of his carriage on her journey
back, for the better accommodation of her sick
child ; and the Colonel, at the joint invitation
of Mrs. Dashwood and Mrs. Jennings, whose

active good-nature made her friendly and hospit-
able for other people as well as herself, engaged
with pleasure to redeem it by a visit at the
cottage in the course of a few weeks.

The day of separation and departure arrived;
and Marianne, after taking so particular and
lengthened a leave of Mrs. Jennings—one so
earnestly grateful, so full of respect and kind
wishes as seemed due to her own heart from a
secret acknowledgment of past inattention—and
bidding Colonel Brandon farewell with the cordiality of a friend, was carefully assisted by him
into the carriage, of which he seemed anxious
that she should engross at least half. Mrs.
Dashwood and Elinor then followed, and the
others were left by themselves, to talk of the
travellers, and feel their own dulness, till Mrs.
Jennings was summoned to her chaise to take
comfort in the gossip of her maid for the loss
of her two young companions; and Colonel
Brandon immediately afterwards took his solitary
way to Delaford.

The Dashwoods were two days on the road,
and Marianne bore her journey on both without
essential fatigue. Everything that the most
zealous affection, the most solicitous care, could
do to render her comfortable, was the office of
each watchful companion, and each found their
reward in her bodily ease and her calmness of

spirits. To Elinor, the observation of the latter was particularly grateful. She who had seen her week after week so constantly suffering, oppressed by anguish of heart which she had neither courage to speak of, nor fortitude to conceal, now saw, with a joy which no other could equally share, an apparent composure of mind which, in being the result, as she trusted, of serious reflection, must eventually lead her to contentment and cheerfulness.

As they approached Barton, indeed, and entered on scenes of which every field and every tree brought some peculiar, some painful recollection, she grew silent and thoughtful, and turning away her face from their notice, sat earnestly gazing through the window. But here, Elinor could neither wonder nor blame; and when she saw, as she assisted Marianne from the carriage, that she had been crying, she saw only an emotion too natural in itself to raise anything less tender than pity, and in its unobtrusiveness entitled to praise. In the whole of her subsequent manner, she traced the direction of a mind awakened to reasonable exertion; for no sooner had they entered their common sitting-room, than Marianne turned her eyes around it with a look of resolute firmness, as if determined at once to accustom herself to the sight of every object with which the

remembrance of Willoughby could be con-
nected. She said little, but every sentence
aimed at cheerfulness, and though a sigh sometimes escaped her, it never passed away without
the atonement of a smile. After dinner, she
would try her pianoforte. She went to it ; but
the music on which her eye first rested was an
opera, procured for her by Willoughby, contain-
ing some of their favourite duets, and bearing
on its outward leaf her own name in his handwriting. That would not do. She shook her
head, put the music aside, and, after running
over the keys for a minute, complained of feebleness in her fingers, and closed the instrument
again ; declaring, however, with firmness as she
did so, that she should in future practise much.

The next morning produced no abatement in
these happy symptoms. On the contrary, with
a mind and body alike strengthened by rest,
she looked and spoke with more genuine spirit,
anticipating the pleasure of Margaret's return,
and talking of the dear family party which
would then be restored, of their mutual pursuits
and cheerful society, as the only happiness worth
a wish.

'When the weather is settled, and I have
recovered my strength,' said she, 'we will take
long walks together every day. We will walk
to the farm at the edge of the down, and see

how the children go on; we will walk to Sir John's new plantations at Barton Cross, and the Abbeyland; and we will often go to the old ruins of the Priory, and try to trace its foundations as far as we are told they once reached. I know we shall be happy. I know the summer will pass happily away. I mean never to be later in rising than six, and from that time till dinner I shall divide every moment between music and reading. I have formed my plan, and am determined to enter on a course of serious study. Our own library is too well known to me to be resorted to for anything beyond mere amusement. But there are many works well worth reading at the Park; and there are others of more modern production which I know I can borrow of Colonel Brandon. By reading only six hours a day, I shall gain in the course of a twelvemonth a great deal of instruction which I now feel myself to want.'

Elinor honoured her for a plan which originated so nobly as this; though smiling to see the same eager fancy which had been leading her to the extreme of languid indolence and selfish repining, now at work in introducing excess into a scheme of such rational employment and virtuous self-controul. Her smile, however, changed to a sigh when she remembered that her promise to Willoughby was yet unfulfilled, and feared she had that to communicate which might again unsettle the mind of Marianne, and ruin, at least for a time, this fair prospect of busy tranquillity. Willing, therefore, to delay the evil hour, she resolved to wait till her sister's health were more secure, before she appointed it. But the resolution was made only to be broken.

Marianne had been two or three days at home before the weather was fine enough for an invalid like herself to venture out. But at last a soft, genial morning appeared—such as might tempt the daughter's wishes and the mother's confidence; and Marianne, leaning on Elinor's arm, was authorised to walk as long as she could without fatigue, in the lane before the house.

The sisters set out at a pace slow as the feebleness of Marianne, in an exercise hitherto untried since her illness, required;—and they had advanced only so far beyond the house as to admit a full view of the hill, the important hill behind, when, pausing with her eyes turned towards it, Marianne calmly said—

'There, exactly there'—pointing with one hand—'on that projecting mound—there I fell; and there I first saw Willoughby.'

Her voice sunk with the word, but presently reviving, she added—

'I am thankful to find that I can look with

2 P*   229

so little pain on the spot!—shall we ever talk on that subject, Elinor?'—hesitatingly it was said.—'Or will it be wrong?—I *can* talk of it now, I hope, as I ought to do.'

Elinor tenderly invited her to be open.

'As for regret,' said Marianne, 'I have done with that, as far as *he* is concerned. I do not mean to talk to you of what my feelings have been for him, but what they are *now*. At present, if I could be satisfied on one point— if I could be allowed to think that he was not *always* acting a part, not *always* deceiving me; but above all, if I could be assured that he never was so *very* wicked as my fears have sometimes fancied him, since the story of that unfortunate girl——'

She stopped. Elinor joyfully treasured her words as she answered—

'If you could be assured of that, you think you should be easy.'

'Yes. My peace of mind is doubly involved in it; for not only is it horrible to suspect a person, who has been what *he* has been to *me*, of such designs—but what must it make me to appear myself? What, in a situation like mine, but a most shamefully unguarded affection could expose me to——'

'How then,' asked her sister, 'would you account for his behaviour?'

'I would suppose him — oh! how gladly would I suppose him—only fickle—very, very fickle.'

Elinor said no more. She was debating within herself on the eligibility of beginning her story directly, or postponing it till Marianne were in stronger health; and they crept on for a few minutes in silence.

'I am not wishing him too much good,' said Marianne at last, with a sigh, 'when I wish his secret reflections may be no more unpleasant than my own. He will suffer enough in them.'

'Do you compare your conduct with his?'

'No. I compare it with what it ought to have been; I compare it with yours.'

'Our situations have borne little resemblance.'

'They have borne more than our conduct. Do not, my dearest Elinor, let your kindness defend what I know your judgment must censure. My illness has made me think—it has given me leisure and calmness for serious recollection. Long before I was enough recovered to talk, I was perfectly able to reflect. I considered the past: I saw in my own behaviour, since the beginning of our acquaintance with him last autumn, nothing but a series of imprudence towards myself, and want of kindness to others. I saw that my own feelings had prepared my sufferings, and that my want of fortitude under them had almost led me to the grave. My illness, I well knew, had been entirely brought on by myself, by such negligence of my own health as I felt even at the time to be wrong. Had I died, it would have been self-destruction. I did not know my danger till the danger was removed ; but with such feelings as these reflections gave me, I wonder at my recovery—wonder that the very eagerness of my desire to live, to have time for atonement to my God, and to you all, did not kill me at once. Had I died, in what peculiar misery should I have left you, my nurse, my friend, my sister ! You, who had seen all the fretful selfishness of my latter days; who had known all the murmurings of my heart ! How should I have lived in *your* remembrance ! My mother too ! How could you have consoled her ! I cannot express my own abhorrence of myself. Whenever I looked towards the past, I saw some duty neglected, or some failing indulged. Everybody seemed injured by me. The kindness, the unceasing kindness of Mrs. Jennings, I had repaid with ungrateful contempt. To the Middletons, the Palmers, the Steeles, to every common acquaintance even, I had been insolent and unjust ; with a heart hardened against their merits, and a temper irritated by their very attention. To

John, to Fanny—yes, even to them, little as
they deserve, I had given less than their due.
But you—you above all, above my mother, had
been wronged by me. I, and only I, knew your
heart and its sorrows; yet, to what did it influence me? not to any compassion that could
benefit you or myself. Your example was
before me; but to what avail? Was I more
considerate of you and your comfort? Did I
imitate your forbearance, or lessen your re-
straints, by taking any part in those offices of
general complaisance or particular gratitude
which you had hitherto been left to discharge
alone? No; not less when I knew you to be
unhappy, than when I had believed you at ease,
did I turn away from every exertion of duty or
friendship; scarcely allowed sorrow to exist but
with me, regretting only *that* heart which de-
serted and wronged me, and leaving you, for
whom I professed an unbounded affection, to be
miserable for my sake.'

Here ceased the rapid flow of her self-reproving
spirit; and Elinor, impatient to soothe, though
too honest to flatter, gave her instantly that
praise and support which her frankness and her
contrition so well deserved. Marianne pressed
her hand and replied—

'You are very good. The future must be my
proof. I have laid down my plan, and if I am

capable of adhering to it, my feelings shall be governed and my temper improved. They shall no longer worry others, nor torture myself. I shall now live solely for my family. You, my mother, and Margaret, must henceforth be all the world to me; you will share my affections entirely between you. From you, from my home, I shall never again have the smallest incitement to move; and if I do mix in other society, it will only be to shew that my spirit is humbled, my heart amended, and that I can practise the civilities, the lesser duties of life, with gentleness and forbearance. As for Willoughby, to say that I shall soon, or that I shall ever forget him, would be idle. His remembrance can be overcome by no change of circumstances or opinions. But it shall be regulated, it shall be checked by religion, by reason, by constant employment.'

She paused, and added in a lower voice, 'If I could but know *his* heart, everything would become easy.'

Elinor, who had now been some time reflecting on the propriety or impropriety of speedily hazarding her narration, without feeling at all nearer decision than at first, heard this; and perceiving that, as reflection did nothing, resolution must do all, soon found herself leading to the fact.

She managed the recital, as she hoped, with
address ; prepared her anxious listener with
caution ; related simply and honestly the chief
points on which Willoughby grounded his
apology ; did justice to his repentance, and
softened only his protestations of present regard.
Marianne said not a word ; she trembled, her
eyes were fixed on the ground, and her lips
became whiter than even sickness had left
them. A thousand inquiries sprang up from
her heart, but she dared not urge one. She
caught every syllable with panting eagerness ; her hand, unknowingly to herself, closely
pressed her sister's, and tears covered her
cheeks.

Elinor, dreading her being tired, led her
towards home ; and till they reached the door
of the cottage, easily conjecturing what her
curiosity must be, though no question was
suffered to speak it, talked of nothing but
Willoughby, and their conversation together
was carefully minute in every particular of speech
and look, where minuteness could be safely indulged. As soon as they entered the house
Marianne, with a kiss of gratitude, and these
two words just articulate through her tears,
' Tell mama,' withdrew from her sister and
walked slowly upstairs. Elinor would not
attempt to disturb a solitude so reasonable as

what she now sought ; and with a mind anxiously prearranging its result, and a resolution of reviving the subject again should Marianne fail to do it, she turned into the parlour to fulfil her parting injunction.

CHAPTER XLVII

MRS. DASHWOOD did not hear unmoved the vindication of her former favourite. She rejoiced in his being cleared from some part of his imputed guilt; she was sorry for him; she wished him happy. But the feelings of the past could not be recalled. Nothing could restore him with a faith unbroken — a character unblemished, to Marianne. Nothing could do away the knowledge of what the latter had suffered through his means, nor remove the guilt of his conduct towards Eliza. Nothing could replace him, therefore, in her former esteem, nor injure the interest of Colonel Brandon.

Had Mrs. Dashwood, like her daughter, heard Willoughby's story from himself—had she witnessed his distress, and been under the influence of his countenance and his manner, it is probable that her compassion would have been greater. But it was neither in Elinor's power, nor in her wish, to rouse such feelings in another, by her retailed explanation, as had at first been called forth in herself. Reflection had given calmness to her judgment, and sobered her own opinion of Willoughby's deserts; she wished, therefore, to declare only the simple truth, and lay open such facts as were really due to his character, without any embellishment of tenderness to lead the fancy astray.

In the evening, when they were all there together, Marianne began voluntarily to speak of him again; but that it was not without an effort, the restless, unquiet thoughtfulness in which she had been for some time previously sitting, her rising colour as she spoke, and her unsteady voice, plainly shewed.

'I wish to assure you both,' said she, 'that I see everything—as you can desire me to do.'

Mrs. Dashwood would have interrupted her instantly with soothing tenderness, had not Elinor, who really wished to hear her sister's unbiassed opinion, by an eager sign, engaged her silence. Marianne slowly continued—

'It is a great relief to me—what Elinor told me this morning—I have now heard exactly what I wished to hear.' For some moments her voice was lost; but, recovering herself, she added, and with greater calmness than before: 'I am now perfectly satisfied. I wish for no change. I never could have been happy with

238

him, after knowing, as sooner or later I must
have known, all this. I should have had no
confidence, no esteem. Nothing could have
done it away to my feelings.'

'I know it—I know it,' cried her mother.
'Happy with a man of libertine practices! With
one who had so injured the peace of the dearest
of our friends, and the best of men? No—my
Marianne has not a heart to be made happy
by such a man! Her conscience, her sensitive
conscience, would have felt all that the conscience
of her husband ought to have felt.'

Marianne sighed, and repeated—'I wish for
no change.'

'You consider the matter,' said Elinor, 'exactly as a good mind and a sound understanding
must consider it; and I dare say you perceive,
as well as myself, not only in this, but in many
other circumstances, reason enough to be convinced that your marriage must have involved
you in many certain troubles and disappointments in which you would have been poorly
supported by an affection, on his side, much less
certain. Had you married, you must have been
always poor. His expensiveness is acknowledged
even by himself, and his whole conduct declares
that self-denial is a word hardly understood by
him. His demands, and your inexperience together, on a small, very small income, must have

brought on distresses which would not be the *less* grievous to you from having been entirely unknown and unthought of before. *Your* sense of honour and honesty would have led you, I know, when aware of your situation, to attempt all the economy that would appear to you possible; and perhaps, as long as your frugality retrenched only on your own comfort, you might have been suffered to practise it, but beyond that—and how little could the utmost of your single management do to stop the ruin which had begun before your marriage? beyond *that*, had you endeavoured, however reasonably, to abridge *his* enjoyments, is it not to be feared that, instead of prevailing on feelings so selfish to consent to it, you would have lessened your own influence on his heart, and made him regret the connexion which had involved him in such difficulties?'

Marianne's lips quivered, and she repeated the word 'Selfish?' in a tone that implied 'Do you really think him selfish?'

'The whole of his behaviour,' replied Elinor, 'from the beginning to the end of the affair, has been grounded on selfishness. It was selfishness which first made him sport with your affections; which afterwards, when his own were engaged, made him delay the confession of it, and which finally carried him from Barton. His own enjoyment, or his own ease, was in every particular his ruling principle.'

'It is very true. *My* happiness never was his object.'

'At present,' continued Elinor, 'he regrets what he has done. And why does he regret it? Because he finds it has not answered towards himself. It has not made him happy. His circumstances are now unembarrassed—he suffers from no evil of that kind, and he thinks only that he has married a woman of a less amiable temper than yourself. But does it thence follow that, had he married you, he would have been happy? The inconveniences would have been different. He would then have suffered under the pecuniary distresses which, because they are removed, he now reckons as nothing. He would have had a wife of whose temper he could make no complaint, but he would have been always necessitous—always poor; and probably would soon have learnt to rank the innumerable comforts of a clear estate and good income as of far more importance, even to domestic happiness, than the mere temper of a wife.'

'I have not a doubt of it,' said Marianne; 'and I have nothing to regret—nothing but my own folly.'

'Rather say your mother's imprudence, my

child,' said Mrs. Dashwood ; '*she* must be answerable.'

Marianne would not let her proceed ; and Elinor, satisfied that each felt their own error, wished to avoid any survey of the past that might weaken her sister's spirits; she therefore, pursuing the first subject, immediately continued—

'*One* observation may, I think, be fairly drawn from the whole of the story—that all Willoughby's difficulties have arisen from the first offence against virtue, in his behaviour to Eliza Williams. That crime has been the origin of every lesser one, and of all his present discontents.'

Marianne assented most feelingly to the remark ; and her mother was led by it to an enumeration of Colonel Brandon's injuries and merits, warm as friendship and design could unitedly dictate. Her daughter did not look, however, as if much of it were heard by her.

Elinor, according to her expectation, saw, on the two or three following days, that Marianne did not continue to gain strength as she had done; but while her resolution was unsubdued, and she still tried to appear cheerful and easy, her sister could safely trust to the effect of time upon her health.

Margaret returned, and the family were again

all restored to each other, again quietly settled at the cottage, and if not pursuing their usual studies with quite so much vigour as when they first came to Barton, at least planning a vigorous prosecution of them in future.

Elinor grew impatient for some tidings of Edward. She had heard nothing of him since her leaving London, nothing new of his plans, nothing certain even of his present abode. Some letters had passed between her and her brother, in consequence of Marianne's illness; and in the first of John's there had been this sentence: 'We know nothing of our unfortunate Edward, and can make no inquiries on so prohibited a subject, but conclude him to be still at Oxford'; which was all the intelligence of Edward afforded her by the correspondence, for his name was not even mentioned in any of the succeeding letters. She was not doomed, however, to be long in ignorance of his measures.

Their man-servant had been sent one morning to Exeter on business; and when, as he waited at table, he had satisfied the inquiries of his mistress as to the event of his errand, this was his voluntary communication—

'I suppose you know, ma'am, that Mr. Ferrars is married.'

Marianne gave a violent start, fixed her eyes upon Elinor, saw her turning pale, and fell back in her chair in hysterics. Mrs. Dashwood, whose eyes, as she answered the servant's inquiry, had intuitively taken the same direction, was shocked to perceive by Elinor's countenance how much she really suffered, and in a moment afterwards, alike distressed by Marianne's situation, knew not on which child to bestow her principal attention.

The servant, who saw only that Miss Marianne was taken ill, had sense enough to call one of the maids, who, with Mrs. Dashwood's assistance, supported her into the other room. By that time Marianne was rather better, and her mother, leaving her to the care of Margaret and the maid, returned to Elinor, who, though still much disordered, had so far recovered the use of her reason and voice as to be just beginning an inquiry of Thomas as to the source of his intelligence. Mrs. Dashwood immediately took all that trouble on herself: and Elinor had the benefit of the information without the exertion of seeking it.

'Who told you that Mr. Ferrars was married, Thomas?'

'I see Mr. Ferrars myself, ma'am, this morning in Exeter, and his lady too, Miss Steele as was. They was stopping in a chaise at the door of the New London Inn, as I went there with a message from Sally at the Park to her brother, who is one of the postboys. I happened to look up as I went by the chaise, and so I see directly it was the youngest Miss Steele; so I took off my hat, and she knew me and called to me, and inquired after you, ma'am, and the young ladies, especially Miss Marianne, and bid me I should give her compliments and Mr. Ferrars's, their best compliments and service, and how sorry they was they had not time to come on and see you—but they was in a great hurry to go forwards, for they was going further down for a little while—but howsever, when they come back, they 'd make sure to come and see you.'

'But did she tell you she was married, Thomas?'

'Yes, ma'am. She smiled, and said how she had changed her name since she was in these parts. She was always a very affable and free-spoken young lady, and very civil-behaved. So, I made free to wish her joy.' ·

'Was Mr. Ferrars in the carriage with her?'

'Yes, ma'am, I just see him leaning back in it, but he did not look up;—he never was a gentleman much for talking.'

Elinor's heart could easily account for his not putting himself forward; and Mrs. Dashwood probably found the same explanation.

'Was there no one else in the carriage?'

'No, ma'am, only they two.'

2 Q*

'Do you know where they came from?'

'They come straight from town, as Miss Lucy
—Mrs. Ferrars told me.'

'And are going farther westward?'

'Yes, ma'am—but not to bide long. They
will soon be back again, and then they'd be
sure and call here.'

Mrs. Dashwood now looked at her daughter;
but Elinor knew better than to expect them.
She recognised the whole of Lucy in the
message, and was very confident that Edward
would never come near them. She observed,
in a low voice, to her mother, that they were
probably going down to Mr. Pratt's, near
Plymouth.

Thomas's intelligence seemed over. Elinor
looked as if she wished to hear more.

'Did you see them off before you came away?'

'No, ma'am—the horses was just coming out,
but I could not bide any longer; I was afraid of
being late.'

'Did Mrs. Ferrars look well?'

'Yes, ma'am, she said how she was very
well; and to my mind she was always a very
handsome young lady—and she seemed vastly
contented.'

Mrs. Dashwood could think of no other
question, and Thomas and the table-cloth, now
alike needless, were soon after dismissed. Mari-

anne had already sent to say that she should eat
nothing more; Mrs. Dashwood's and Elinor's
appetites were equally lost, and Margaret might
think herself very well off, that with so much
uneasiness as both her sisters had lately experienced, so much reason as they had often had to
be careless of their meals, she had never been
obliged to go without her dinner before.

When the dessert and the wine were arranged,
and Mrs. Dashwood and Elinor were left to
themselves, they remained long together in a
similarity of thoughtfulness and silence. Mrs.
Dashwood feared to hazard any remark, and
ventured not to offer consolation. She now
found that she had erred in relying on Elinor's
representation of herself; and justly concluded
that everything had been expressly softened at
the time, to spare her from an increase of unhappiness, suffering as she then had suffered
for Marianne. She found that she had been
misled by the careful, the considerate attention
of her daughter, to think the attachment, which
once she had so well understood, much slighter
in reality than she had been wont to believe, or
than it was now proved to be. She feared that
under this persuasion she had been unjust, in-
attentive—nay, almost unkind to her Elinor:
that Marianne's affliction, because more acknowledged, more immediately before her, had too

much engrossed her tenderness, and led her away to forget that in Elinor she might have a daughter suffering almost as much, certainly with less self-provocation and greater fortitude.

CHAPTER XLVIII

ELINOR now found the difference between the expectation of an unpleasant event, however certain the mind may be told to consider it, and certainty itself. She now found that, in spite of herself, she had always admitted a hope, while Edward remained single, that something would occur to prevent his marrying Lucy ; that some resolution of his own, some mediation of friends, or some more eligible opportunity of establishment for the lady, would arise to assist the happiness of all. But he was now married, and she condemned her heart for the lurking flattery which so much heightened the pain of the intelligence.

That he should be married so soon, before (as she imagined) he could be in orders, and consequently before he could be in possession of the living, surprised her a little at first. But she soon saw how likely it was that Lucy, in her self-provident care, in her haste to secure him, should overlook everything but the risk of delay.

They were married, married in town, and now hastening down to her uncle's. What had Edward felt on being within four miles of Barton, on seeing her mother's servant, on hearing Lucy's message!

They would soon, she supposed, be settled at Delaford—Delaford, that place in which so much conspired to give her an interest—which she wished to be acquainted with, and yet desired to avoid. She saw them in an instant in their parsonage-house; saw in Lucy the active, contriving manager, uniting at once a desire of smart appearance with the utmost frugality, and ashamed to be suspected of half her economical practices;—pursuing her own interest in every thought, courting the favour of Colonel Brandon, of Mrs. Jennings, and of every wealthy friend. In Edward she knew not what she saw, nor what she wished to see;—happy or unhappy—nothing pleased her;—she turned away her head from every sketch of him.

Elinor flattered herself that some one of their connexions in London would write to them to announce the event, and give farther particulars; but day after day passed off, and brought no letter, no tidings. Though uncertain that any one were to blame, she found fault with every absent friend. They were all thoughtless or indolent.

SENSE AND SENSIBILITY

'When do you write to Colonel Brandon, ma'am?' was an inquiry which sprung from the impatience of her mind to have something going on.

'I wrote to him, my love, last week, and rather expect to see, than to hear from him again. I earnestly pressed his coming to us, and should not be surprised to see him walk in to-day or to-morrow, or any day.'

This was gaining something, something to look forward to. Colonel Brandon *must* have some information to give.

Scarcely had she so determined it, when the figure of a man on horseback drew her eyes to the window. He stopped at their gate. It was a gentleman, it was Colonel Brandon himself. Now she should hear more;—and she trembled in expectation of it. But—it was *not* Colonel Brandon—neither his air nor his height. Were it possible, she should say it must be Edward. She looked again. He had just dismounted;— she could not be mistaken—it *was* Edward. She moved away and sat down. 'He comes from Mr. Pratt's purposely to see us. I *will* be calm; I *will* be mistress of myself.'

In a moment she perceived that the others were likewise aware of the mistake. She saw her mother and Marianne change colour; saw them look at herself, and whisper a few sentences

to each other. She would have given the world
to be able to speak—and to make them understand that she hoped no coolness, no slight,
would appear in their behaviour to him ; but
she had no utterance, and was obliged to leave
all to their own discretion.

Not a syllable passed aloud. They all waited
in silence for the appearance of their visitor.
His footsteps were heard along the gravel path ;
in a moment he was in the passage, and in
another he was before them.

His countenance, as he entered the room, was
not too happy, even for Elinor. His complexion
was white with agitation, and he looked as if
fearful of his reception, and conscious that he
merited no kind one. Mrs. Dashwood, however, conforming, as she trusted, to the wishes
of that daughter by whom she then meant, in
the warmth of her heart, to be guided in everything, met him with a look of forced complacency,
gave him her hand, and wished him joy.

He coloured, and stammered out an un-
intelligible reply. Elinor's lips had moved with
her mother's, and when the moment of action
was over, she wished that she had shaken hands
with him too. But it was then too late, and
with a countenance meaning to be open, she
sat down again and talked of the weather.

Marianne had retreated as much as possible out

of sight, to conceal her distress; and Margaret, understanding some part, but not the whole of the case, thought it incumbent on her to be dignified, and therefore took a seat as far from him as she could, and maintained a strict silence.

When Elinor had ceased to rejoice in the dryness of the season, a very awful pause took place. It was put an end to by Mrs. Dashwood, who felt obliged to hope that he had left Mrs. Ferrars very well. In a hurried manner he replied in the affirmative.

Another pause.

Elinor, resolving to exert herself, though fearing the sound of her own voice, now said—

'Is Mrs. Ferrars at Longstaple?'

'At Longstaple!' he replied, with an air of surprise. 'No, my mother is in town.'

'I meant,' said Elinor, taking up some work from the table, 'to inquire after Mrs. *Edward* Ferrars.'

She dared not look up;—but her mother and Marianne both turned their eyes on him. He coloured, seemed perplexed, looked doubtingly, and after some hesitation, said—

'Perhaps you mean—my brother—you mean Mrs.—Mrs. *Robert* Ferrars.'

'Mrs. Robert Ferrars!' was repeated by Marianne and her mother in an accent of the utmost amazement; and though Elinor could not speak, even *her* eyes were fixed on him with the same impatient wonder. He rose from his seat and walked to the window, apparently from not knowing what to do; took up a pair of scissors that lay there, and while spoiling both them and their sheath by cutting the latter to pieces as he spoke, said, in an hurried voice—

'Perhaps you do not know—you may not have heard that my brother is lately married to —to the youngest—to Miss Lucy Steele.'

His words were echoed with unspeakable astonishment by all but Elinor, who sat with her head leaning over her work, in a state of such agitation as made her hardly know where she was.

'Yes,' said he, 'they were married last week and are now at Dawlish.'

Elinor could sit it no longer. She almost ran out of the room, and as soon as the door was closed, burst into tears of joy, which at first she thought would never cease. Edward, who had till then looked anywhere rather than at her, saw her hurry away, and perhaps saw—or even heard—her emotion; for immediately afterwards he fell into a reverie, which no remarks, no inquiries, no affectionate address of Mrs. Dashwood could penetrate, and at last, without saying a word, quitted the room, and walked out towards the village, leaving the others in the greatest astonishment and perplexity on a change in his situation so wonderful and so sudden—a perplexity which they had no means of lessening but by their own conjectures.

CHAPTER XLIX

UNACCOUNTABLE, however, as the circumstances of his release might appear to the whole family, it was certain that Edward was free; and to what purpose that freedom would be employed was easily predetermined by all; for after experiencing the blessings of *one* imprudent engagement, contracted without his mother's consent, as he had already done for more than four years, nothing less could be expected of him in the failure of *that*, than the immediate contraction of another.

His errand at Barton, in fact, was a simple one. It was only to ask Elinor to marry him; and considering that he was not altogether inexperienced in such a question, it might be strange that he should feel so uncomfortable in the present case as he really did, so much in need of encouragement and fresh air.

How soon he had walked himself into the proper resolution, however, how soon an opportunity of exercising it occurred, in what manner he expressed himself, and how he was received,

256

need not be particularly told. This only need be said :—that when they all sat down to table at four o'clock, about three hours after his arrival, he had secured his lady, engaged her mother's consent, and was not only in the rapturous profession of the lover, but in the reality of reason and truth, one of the happiest of men. His situation indeed was more than commonly joyful. He had more than the ordinary triumph of accepted love to swell his heart and raise his spirits. He was released, without any reproach to himself, from an entanglement which had long formed his misery, from a woman whom he had long ceased to love—and elevated at once to that security with another, which he must have thought of almost with despair, as soon as he had learnt to consider it with desire. He was brought, not from doubt or suspense, but from misery to happiness ; and the change was openly spoken in such a genuine, flowing, grateful cheerfulness, as his friends had never witnessed in him before.

His heart was now open to Elinor—all its weaknesses, all its errors confessed, and his first boyish attachment to Lucy treated with all the philosophic dignity of twenty-four.

'It was a foolish, idle inclination on my side,' said he, 'the consequence of ignorance of the world—and want of employment. Had my

mother given me some active profession when
I was removed at eighteen from the care of
Mr. Pratt, I think, nay, I am sure, it would
never have happened; for, though I left Longstaple with what I thought, at the time, a most
unconquerable preference for his niece, yet had
I then had any pursuit, any object to engage
my time and keep me at a distance from her for
a few months, I should very soon have out-
grown the fancied attachment, especially by
mixing more with the world, as in such a case
I must have done. But instead of having anything to do—instead of having any profession
chosen for me, or being allowed to chuse any
myself, I returned home to be completely idle;
and for the first twelvemonth afterwards I had
not even the nominal employment which belong-
ing to the university would have given me, for
I was not entered at Oxford till I was nineteen.
I had therefore nothing in the world to do but
to fancy myself in love; and as my mother did
not make my home in every respect comfortable,
as I had no friend, no companion in my brother,
and disliked new acquaintance, it was not unnatural for me to be very often at Longstaple,
where I always felt myself at home, and was
always sure of a welcome; and accordingly I
spent the greatest part of my time there from
eighteen to nineteen. Lucy appeared every-

thing that was amiable and obliging. She was pretty too—at least I thought so *then*; and I had seen so little of other women that I could make no comparisons, and see no defects. Considering everything, therefore, I hope, foolish as our engagement was, foolish as it has since in every way been proved, it was not at the time an unnatural, or an inexcusable piece of folly.'

The change which a few hours had wrought in the minds and the happiness of the Dashwoods was such—so great—as promised them all the satisfaction of a sleepless night. Mrs. Dashwood, too happy to be comfortable, knew not how to love Edward nor praise Elinor enough—how to be enough thankful for his release without wounding his delicacy, nor how at once to give them leisure for unrestrained conversation together, and yet enjoy, as she wished, the sight and society of both.

Marianne could speak *her* happiness only by tears. Comparisons would occur, regrets would arise; and her joy, though sincere as her love for her sister, was of a kind to give her neither spirits nor language.

But Elinor, how are *her* feelings to be described? From the moment of learning that Lucy was married to another, that Edward was free, to the moment of his justifying the hopes which had so instantly followed, she was every-

thing by turns but tranquil. But when the
second moment had passed—when she found
every doubt, every solicitude removed—com-
pared her situation with what so lately it had
been—saw him honourably released from his
former engagement—saw him instantly profiting
by the release, to address herself and declare an
affection as tender, as constant as she had ever
supposed it to be—she was oppressed, she was
overcome by her own felicity; and happily disposed as is the human mind to be easily familiar-
ised with any change for the better, it required
several hours to give sedateness to her spirits, or
any degree of tranquillity to her heart.

Edward was now fixed at the cottage at least
for a week; for whatever other claims might be
made on him, it was impossible that less than a
week should be given up to the enjoyment of
Elinor's company, or suffice to say half that was
to be said of the past, the present, and the
future; for though a very few hours spent in the
hard labour of incessant talking will despatch
more subjects than can really be in common
between any two rational creatures, yet with
lovers it is different. Between *them* no subject
is finished, no communication is even made, till
it has been made at least twenty times over.

Lucy's marriage, the unceasing and reasonable
wonder among them all, formed of course one

of the earliest discussions of the lovers; and
Elinor's particular knowledge of each party
made it appear to her, in every view, as one
of the most extraordinary and unaccountable
circumstances she had ever heard. How they
could be thrown together, and by what attraction Robert could be drawn on to marry a girl
of whose beauty she had herself heard him speak
without any admiration — a girl, too, already
engaged to his brother, and on whose account
that brother had been thrown off by his family—
it was beyond her comprehension to make out.
To her own heart it was a delightful affair, to
her imagination it was even a ridiculous one;
but to her reason, her judgment, it was completely a puzzle.

Edward could only attempt an explanation by
supposing that, perhaps, at first accidentally
meeting, the vanity of the one had been so
worked on by the flattery of the other as to
lead by degrees to all the rest. Elinor remembered what Robert had told her in Harley
Street, of his opinion of what his own mediation
in his brother's affairs might have done, if applied
to in time. She repeated it to Edward.

'*That* was exactly like Robert,' was his
immediate observation. 'And *that*,' he presently
added, 'might perhaps be in *his* head when the
acquaintance between them first began. And

2 R*   261

Lucy, perhaps, at first might think only of procuring his good offices in my favour. Other designs might afterwards arise.'

How long it had been carrying on between them, however, he was equally at a loss with herself to make out; for at Oxford, where he had remained by choice ever since his quitting London, he had had no means of hearing of her but from herself, and her letters to the very last were neither less frequent nor less affectionate than usual. Not the smallest suspicion, therefore, had ever occurred to prepare him for what followed; and when at last it burst on him in a letter from Lucy herself, he had been for some time, he believed, half stupefied between the wonder, the horror, and the joy, of such a deliverance. He put the letter into Elinor's hands—

'DEAR SIR,—Being very sure I have long lost your affections, I have thought myself at liberty to bestow my own on another, and have no doubt of being as happy with him as I once used to think I might be with you; but I scorn to accept a hand while the heart was another's. Sincerely wish you happy in your choice, and it shall not be my fault if we are not always good friends, as our near relationship now makes proper. I can safely say I owe you no ill-will, and am sure you will be too generous to do us any ill offices. Your brother has gained my affections entirely, and as we could not live without one another, we are just returned from the altar, and are now on our way to Dawlish for a few weeks, which place your dear brother has great curiosity to see, but thought I would first trouble you with these few lines, and shall always remain,—Your sincere well-wisher, friend, and sister,   LUCY FERRARS.

'I have burnt all your letters, and will return your picture the first opportunity. Please to destroy my scrawls; but the ring, with my hair, you are very welcome to keep.'

Elinor read and returned it without any comment.

'I will not ask your opinion of it as a composition,' said Edward. 'For worlds would not I have had a letter of hers seen by *you* in former days. In a sister it is bad enough, but in a wife! How I have blushed over the pages of her writing! and I believe I may say that since the first half-year of our foolish—business —this is the only letter I ever received from her, of which the substance made me any amends for the defect of the style.'

'However it may have come about,' said Elinor, after a pause, 'they are certainly married. And your mother has brought on herself a most appropriate punishment. The independence she settled on Robert, through resentment against you, has put it in his power to make his own choice; and she has actually been bribing one son with a thousand a year to do the very deed which she disinherited the other for intending to do. She will hardly be less hurt, I suppose, by Robert's marrying Lucy, than she would have been by your marrying her.'

'She will be more hurt by it, for Robert always was her favourite. She will be more hurt by it, and on the same principle will forgive him much sooner.'

In what state the affair stood at present between them Edward knew not, for no communication with any of his family had yet been attempted by him. He had quitted Oxford within four-and-twenty hours after Lucy's letter arrived, and with only one object before him, the nearest road to Barton, had had no leisure to form any scheme of conduct with which that road did not hold the most intimate connexion. He could do nothing till he were assured of his fate with Miss Dashwood; and by his rapidity in seeking *that* fate, it is to be supposed, in spite of the jealousy with which he had once thought of Colonel Brandon—in spite of the modesty with which he rated his own deserts,

and the politeness with which he talked of his
doubts, he did not upon the whole expect a very
cruel reception. It was his business, however,
to say that he *did*, and he said it very prettily.
What he might say on the subject a twelvemonth after, must be referred to the imagination of husbands and wives.

That Lucy had certainly meant to deceive, to
go off with a flourish of malice against him in
her message by Thomas, was perfectly clear to
Elinor; and Edward himself, now thoroughly
enlightened on her character, had no scruple in
believing her capable of the utmost meanness of
wanton ill-nature. Though his eyes had been
long opened, even before his acquaintance with
Elinor began, to her ignorance and a want of
liberality in some of her opinions, they had been
equally imputed by him to her want of education; and till her last letter reached him he had
always believed her to be a well-disposed, good-
hearted girl, and thoroughly attached to himself.
Nothing but such a persuasion could have prevented his putting an end to an engagement
which, long before the discovery of it laid him
open to his mother's anger, had been a continual
source of disquiet and regret to him.

'I thought it my duty,' said he, 'independent
of my feelings, to give her the option of continuing the engagement or not, when I was

renounced by my mother, and stood to all appearance without a friend in the world to assist me. In such a situation as that, where there seemed nothing to tempt the avarice or the vanity of any living creature, how could I suppose, when she so earnestly, so warmly insisted on sharing my fate, whatever it might be, that anything but the most disinterested affection was her inducement? And even now I cannot comprehend on what motive she acted, or what fancied advantage it could be to her, to be fettered to a man for whom she had not the smallest regard, and who had only two thousand pounds in the world. She could not foresee that Colonel Brandon would give me a living.'

'No, but she might suppose that something would occur in your favour; that your own family might in time relent. And at any rate, she lost nothing by continuing the engagement, for she has proved that it fettered neither her inclination nor her actions. The connexion was certainly a respectable one, and probably gained her consideration among her friends; and if nothing more advantageous occurred, it would be better for her to marry *you* than be single.'

Edward was of course immediately convinced that nothing could have been more natural than Lucy's conduct, nor more self-evident than the motive of it.

SENSE AND SENSIBILITY

Elinor scolded him, harshly as ladies always scold the imprudence which compliments themselves, for having spent so much time with them at Norland, when he must have felt his own inconstancy.

'Your behaviour was certainly very wrong,' said she, 'because—to say nothing of my own conviction—our relations were all led away by it to fancy and expect *what*, as you were *then* situated, could never be.'

He could only plead an ignorance of his own heart, and a mistaken confidence in the force of his engagement.

'I was simple enough to think that, because my *faith* was plighted to another, there could be no danger in my being with you; and that the consciousness of my engagement was to keep my heart as safe and sacred as my honour. I felt that I admired you, but I told myself it was only friendship; and till I began to make comparisons between yourself and Lucy, I did not know how far I was got. After that, I suppose, I *was* wrong in remaining so much in Sussex, and the arguments with which I reconciled myself to the expediency of it were no better than these :—The danger is my own; I am doing no injury to anybody but myself.'

Elinor smiled and shook her head.

Edward heard with pleasure of Colonel

Brandon's being expected at the cottage, as he really wished not only to be better acquainted with him, but to have an opportunity of convincing him that he no longer resented his giving him the living of Delaford—'Which at present,' said he, 'after thanks so ungraciously delivered as mine were on the occasion, he must think I have never forgiven him for offering.'

Now he felt astonished himself that he had never yet been to the place. But so little interest had he taken in the matter, that he owed all his knowledge of the house, garden, and glebe, extent of the parish, condition of the land, and rate of the tithes, to Elinor herself, who had heard so much of it from Colonel Brandon, and heard it with so much attention as to be entirely mistress of the subject.

One question after this only remained undecided between them, one difficulty only was to be overcome. They were brought together by mutual affection, with the warmest approbation of their real friends; their intimate knowledge of each other seemed to make their happiness certain—and they only wanted something to live upon. Edward had two thousand pounds, and Elinor one, which, with Delaford living, was all that they could call their own; for it was impossible that Mrs. Dashwood should advance anything, and they

were neither of them quite enough in love to
think that three hundred and fifty pounds a
year would supply them with the comforts of
life.

Edward was not entirely without hopes of
some favourable change in his mother towards
him ; and on *that* he rested for the residue of
their income. But Elinor had no such dependence ; for, since Edward would still be unable
to marry Miss Morton, and his chusing herself
had been spoken of in Mrs. Ferrars's flattering
language as only a lesser evil than his chusing
Lucy Steele, she feared that Robert's offence
would serve no other purpose than to enrich
Fanny.

About four days after Edward's arrival
Colonel Brandon appeared, to complete Mrs.
Dashwood's satisfaction, and to give her the
dignity of having, for the first time since her
living at Barton, more company with her than
her house would hold. Edward was allowed to
retain the privilege of first-comer, and Colonel
Brandon therefore walked every night to his
old quarters at the Park ; from whence he
usually returned in the morning, early enough
to interrupt the lovers' first *tête-à-tête* before
breakfast.

A three weeks' residence at Delaford, where,
in his evening hours at least, he had little to

do but to calculate the disproportion between thirty-six and seventeen, brought him to Barton in a temper of mind which needed all the improvement in Marianne's looks, all the kindness of her welcome, and all the encouragement of her mother's language, to make it cheerful. Among such friends, however, and such flattery, he did revive. No rumour of Lucy's marriage had yet reached him ; he knew nothing of what had passed, and the first hours of his visit were consequently spent in hearing and in wondering. Everything was explained to him by Mrs. Dashwood, and he found fresh reason to rejoice in what he had done for Mr. Ferrars, since eventually it promoted the interest of Elinor.

It would be needless to say that the gentlemen advanced in the good opinion of each other as they advanced in each other's acquaintance, for it could not be otherwise. Their resemblance in good principles and good sense, in disposition and manner of thinking, would probably have been sufficient to unite them in friendship, without any other attraction ; but their being in love with two sisters, and two sisters fond of each other, made that mutual regard inevitable and immediate, which might otherwise have waited the effect of time and judgment.

The letters from town, which a few days before would have made every nerve in Elinor's body thrill with transport, now arrived to be read with less emotion than mirth. Mrs. Jennings wrote to tell the wonderful tale, to vent her honest indignation against the jilting girl, and pour forth her compassion towards poor Mr. Edward, who, she was sure, had quite doated upon the worthless hussy, and was now, by all accounts, almost broken-hearted, at Oxford.— 'I do think,' she continued, 'nothing was ever carried on so sly; for it was but two days before Lucy called and sat a couple of hours with me. Not a soul suspected anything of the matter, not even Nancy, who, poor soul! came crying to me the day after, in a great fright for fear of Mrs. Ferrars, as well as not knowing how to get to Plymouth; for Lucy, it seems, borrowed all her money before she went off to be married, on purpose, we suppose, to make a show with, and poor Nancy had not seven shillings in the world; —so I was very glad to give her five guineas, to take her down to Exeter, where she thinks of staying three or four weeks with Mrs. Burgess, in hopes, as I tell her, to fall in with the doctor again. And I must say that Lucy's crossness not to take her along with them in the chaise is worse than all. Poor Mr. Edward! I cannot get him out of my head, but you must send for him to Barton, and Miss Marianne must try to comfort him.'

271

Mr. Dashwood's strains were more solemn. Mrs. Ferrars was the most unfortunate of women —poor Fanny had suffered agonies of sensibility—and he considered the existence of each, under such a blow, with grateful wonder. Robert's offence was unpardonable, but Lucy's was infinitely worse. Neither of them was ever again to be mentioned to Mrs. Ferrars; and, even if she might hereafter be induced to forgive her son, his wife should never be acknowledged as her daughter, nor be permitted to appear in her presence. The secrecy with which everything had been carried on between them was rationally treated as enormously heightening the crime, because, had any suspicion of it occurred to the others, proper measures would have been taken to prevent the marriage; and he called on Elinor to join with him in regretting that Lucy's engagement with Edward had not rather been fulfilled, than that she should thus be the means of spreading misery farther in the family. He thus continued—

'Mrs. Ferrars has never yet mentioned Edward's name, which does not surprise us; but, to our great astonishment, not a line has been received from him on the occasion. Perhaps, however, he is kept silent by his fear of offending, and I shall therefore give him a hint, by a line to Oxford, that his sister and I both think a letter of proper submission from him, addressed perhaps to Fanny, and by her shewn to her mother, might not be taken amiss; for we all know the tenderness of Mrs. Ferrars's heart, and that she wishes for nothing so much as to be on good terms with her children.'

This paragraph was of some importance to the prospects and conduct of Edward. It determined him to attempt a reconciliation, though not exactly in the manner pointed out by their brother and sister.

'A letter of proper submission!' repeated he; 'would they have me beg my mother's pardon for Robert's ingratitude to *her*, and breach of honour to *me*?—I can make no submission—I am grown neither humble nor penitent by what has passed. I am grown very happy, but that would not interest. I know of no submission that *is* proper for me to make.'

'You may certainly ask to be forgiven,' said Elinor, 'because you have offended; and I should think you might *now* venture so far as to profess some concern for having ever formed the engagement which drew on you your mother's anger.'

He agreed that he might.

'And when she has forgiven you, perhaps a little humility may be convenient while acknowledging a second engagement, almost as imprudent in *her* eyes as the first.'

He had nothing to urge against it, but still resisted the idea of a letter of proper submission; and therefore, to make it easier to him, as he declared a much greater willingness to make mean concessions by word of mouth than on paper, it was resolved that, instead of writing to Fanny, he should go to London, and personally entreat her good offices in his favour. 'And if they really *do* interest themselves,' said Marianne, in her new character of candour, 'in bringing about a reconciliation, I shall think that even John and Fanny are not entirely without merit.'

After a visit on Colonel Brandon's side of only three or four days, the two gentlemen quitted Barton together. They were to go immediately to Delaford, that Edward might have some personal knowledge of his future home, and assist his patron and friend in deciding on what improvements were needed to it; and from thence, after staying there a couple of nights, he was to proceed on his journey to town.

CHAPTER L

AFTER a proper resistance on the part of Mrs. Ferrars, just so violent and so steady as to preserve her from that reproach which she always seemed fearful of incurring, the reproach of being too amiable, Edward was admitted to her presence, and pronounced to be again her son.

Her family had of late been exceedingly fluctuating. For many years of her life she had had two sons; but the crime and annihilation of Edward, a few weeks ago, had robbed her of one; the similar annihilation of Robert had left her for a fortnight without any; and now, by the resuscitation of Edward, she had one again.

In spite of his being allowed once more to live, however, he did not feel the continuance of his existence secure, till he had revealed his present engagement; for the publication of that circumstance, he feared, might give a sudden turn to his constitution, and carry him off as rapidly as before. With apprehensive caution, therefore, it was revealed, and he was listened to with unexpected calmness. Mrs. Ferrars at first reasonably endeavoured to dissuade him from marrying Miss Dashwood, by every argument in her power;—told him, that in Miss Morton he would have a woman of higher rank and larger fortune;—and enforced the assertion by observing that Miss Morton was the daughter of a nobleman with thirty thousand pounds, while Miss Dashwood was only the daughter of a private gentleman, with no more than *three*; but when she found that, though perfectly admitting the truth of her representation, he was by no means inclined to be guided by it, she judged it wisest, from the experience of the past, to submit—and therefore, after such an ungracious delay as she owed to her own dignity, and as served to prevent every suspicion of goodwill, she issued her decree of consent to the marriage of Edward and Elinor.

What she would engage to do towards augmenting their income was next to be considered : and here it plainly appeared, that though Edward was now her only son, he was by no means her eldest; for while Robert was inevitably endowed with a thousand pounds a year, not the smallest objection was made against Edward's taking orders for the sake of two hundred and fifty at the utmost; nor was anything promised either for the present or in future, beyond the ten thousand pounds, which had been given with Fanny.

It was as much, however, as was desired, and more than was expected, by Edward and Elinor; and Mrs. Ferrars herself, by her shuffling excuses, seemed the only person surprised at her not giving more.

With an income quite sufficient to their wants thus secured to them, they had nothing to wait for, after Edward was in possession of the living, but the readiness of the house, to which Colonel Brandon, with an eager desire for the accommodation of Elinor, was making considerable improvements; and after waiting some time for their completion—after experiencing, as usual, a thousand disappointments and delays, from the unaccountable dilatoriness of the workmen —Elinor, as usual, broke through the first positive resolution of not marrying till everything was ready, and the ceremony took place in Barton church early in the autumn.

The first month after their marriage was spent with their friend at the mansion-house, from whence they could superintend the progress of the parsonage, and direct everything as they liked on the spot; could chuse papers, project shrubberies, and invent a sweep. Mrs. Jennings's prophecies, though rather jumbled together,

were chiefly fulfilled; for she was able to visit
Edward and his wife in their parsonage by
Michaelmas, and she found in Elinor and her
husband, as she really believed, one of the
happiest couples in the world. They had
in fact nothing to wish for, but the marriage
of Colonel Brandon and Marianne, and rather
better pasturage for their cows.

They were visited on their first settling by
almost all their relations and friends. Mrs.
Ferrars came to inspect the happiness which she
was almost ashamed of having authorised; and
even the Dashwoods were at the expense of a
journey from Sussex to do them honour.

'I will not say that I am disappointed, my
dear sister,' said John, as they were walking
together one morning before the gates of Delaford House—'*that* would be saying too much,
for certainly you have been one of the most
fortunate young women in the world, as it is.
But, I confess, it would give me great pleasure
to call Colonel Brandon brother. His property
here, his place, his house, everything in such
respectable and excellent condition! and his
woods! I have not seen such timber anywhere
in Dorsetshire as there is now standing in Delaford Hanger! And though, perhaps, Marianne
may not seem exactly the person to attract him,
yet I think it would altogether be advisable for

278

you to have them now frequently staying with you; for as Colonel Brandon seems a great deal at home, nobody can tell what may happen—for, when people are much thrown together, and see little of anybody else—and it will always be in your power to set her off to advantage, and so forth; in short, you may as well give her a chance—You understand me.'

But though Mrs. Ferrars *did* come to see them, and always treated them with the make-believe of decent affection, they were never insulted by her real favour and preference. *That* was due to the folly of Robert, and the cunning of his wife; and it was earned by them before many months had passed away. The selfish sagacity of the latter, which had at first drawn Robert into the scrape, was the principal instrument of his deliverance from it; for her respectful humility, assiduous attentions, and endless flatteries, as soon as the smallest opening was given for their exercise, reconciled Mrs. Ferrars to his choice, and re-established him completely in her favour.

The whole of Lucy's behaviour in the affair, and the prosperity which crowned it, therefore, may be held forth as a most encouraging instance of what an earnest, an unceasing attention to self-interest, however its progress may be apparently obstructed, will do in securing

every advantage of fortune, with no other
sacrifice than that of time and conscience.
When Robert first sought her acquaintance,
and privately visited her in Bartlett's Buildings,
it was only with the view imputed to him by
his brother. He merely meant to persuade her
to give up the engagement; and as there could
be nothing to overcome but the affection of
both, he naturally expected that one or two
interviews would settle the matter. In that
point, however, and that only, he erred; for
though Lucy soon gave him hopes that his
eloquence would convince her in *time*, another
visit, another conversation, was always wanted
to produce this conviction. Some doubts always
lingered in her mind when they parted, which
could only be removed by another half-hour's
discourse with himself. His attendance was by
this means secured, and the rest followed in
course. Instead of talking of Edward, they
came gradually to talk only of Robert, a subject
on which he had always more to say than on
any other, and in which she soon betrayed an
interest even equal to his own; and in short,
it became speedily evident to both, that he had
entirely supplanted his brother. He was proud
of his conquest, proud of tricking Edward, and
very proud of marrying privately without his
mother's consent. What immediately followed

is known. They passed some months in great
happiness at Dawlish ; for she had many relations
and old acquaintance to cut—and he drew several
plans for magnificent cottages ; and from thence
returning to town, procured the forgiveness of
Mrs. Ferrars, by the simple expedient of asking
it, which, at Lucy's instigation, was adopted.
The forgiveness at first, indeed, as was reasonable, comprehended only Robert ; and Lucy,
who had owed his mother no duty, and therefore could have transgressed none, still remained
some weeks longer unpardoned. But persever-
ance in humility of conduct, and messages, in
self-condemnation for Robert's offence, and
gratitude for the unkindness she was treated
with, procured her in time the haughty notice
which overcame her by its graciousness, and led
soon afterwards, by rapid degrees, to the highest
state of affection and influence. Lucy became
as necessary to Mrs. Ferrars as either Robert or
Fanny ; and while Edward was never cordially
forgiven for having once intended to marry her,
and Elinor, though superior to her in fortune
and birth, was spoken of as an intruder, *she* was
in everything considered, and always openly
acknowledged, to be a favourite child. They
settled in town, received very liberal assistance
from Mrs. Ferrars, were on the best terms
imaginable with the Dashwoods, and setting

aside the jealousies and ill-will continually sub-
sisting between Fanny and Lucy, in which their
husbands of course took a part, as well as the
frequent domestic disagreements between Robert
and Lucy themselves, nothing could exceed the
harmony in which they all lived together.

What Edward had done to forfeit the right
of eldest son might have puzzled many people
to find out; and what Robert had done to
succeed to it might have puzzled them still
more. It was an arrangement, however, justified
in its effects, if not in its cause; for nothing ever
appeared in Robert's style of living, or of talking, to give a suspicion of his regretting the
extent of his income, as either leaving his
brother too little, or bringing himself too much;
and if Edward might be judged from the ready
discharge of his duties in every particular, from
an increasing attachment to his wife and his
home, and from the regular cheerfulness of his
spirits, he might be supposed no less contented
with his lot, no less free from every wish of an
exchange.

Elinor's marriage divided her as little from her
family as could well be contrived, without
rendering the cottage at Barton entirely useless,
for her mother and sisters spent much more than
half their time with her. Mrs. Dashwood was
acting on motives of policy as well as pleasure

in the frequency of her visits to Delaford; for her wish of bringing Marianne and Colonel Brandon together was hardly less earnest, though rather more liberal, than what John had expressed. It was now her darling object. Precious as was the company of her daughter to her, she desired nothing so much as to give up its constant enjoyment to her valued friend; and to see Marianne settled at the mansion-house was equally the wish of Edward and Elinor. They each felt his sorrows and their own obligations, and Marianne, by general consent, was to be the reward of all.

With such a confederacy against her—with a knowledge so intimate of his goodness—with a conviction of his fond attachment to herself, which at last, though long after it was observable to everybody else, burst on her — what could she do?

Marianne Dashwood was born to an extra-ordinary fate. She was born to discover the falsehood of her own opinions and to counteract by her conduct her most favourite maxims. She was born to overcome an affection formed so late in life as at seventeen, and with no sentiment superior to strong esteem and lively friendship, voluntarily to give her hand to another! and *that* other, a man who had suffered no less than herself under the event of a former attachment—whom, two years before, she had considered too old to be married—and who still sought the constitutional safeguard of a flannel waistcoat!

But so it was. Instead of falling a sacrifice to an irresistible passion, as once she had fondly flattered herself with expecting—instead of remaining even for ever with her mother, and finding her only pleasures in retirement and study, as afterwards in her more calm and sober judgment she had determined on—she found herself, at nineteen, submitting to new attachments, entering on new duties, placed in a new home, a wife, the mistress of a family, and the patroness of a village.

Colonel Brandon was now as happy as all those who best loved him believed he deserved to be ; in Marianne he was consoled for every past affliction ; her regard and her society restored his mind to animation, and his spirits to cheerfulness : and that Marianne found her own happiness in forming his, was equally the persuasion and delight of each observing friend. Marianne could never love by halves ; and her whole heart became, in time, as much devoted to her husband as it had once been to Willoughby.

Willoughby could not hear of her marriage without a pang ; and his punishment was soon afterwards complete in the voluntary forgiveness of Mrs. Smith, who, by stating his marriage with a woman of character as the source of her clemency, gave him reason for believing that, had he behaved with honour towards Marianne, he might at once have been happy and rich. That his repentance of misconduct, which thus brought its own punishment, was sincere, need not be doubted; nor that he long thought of Colonel Brandon with envy, and of Marianne with regret. But that he was for ever inconsolable—that he fled from society, or contracted an habitual gloom of temper, or died of a broken heart, must not be depended on—for he did neither. He lived to exert, and frequently to enjoy himself. His wife was not always out of humour, nor his home always uncomfortable! and in his breed of horses and dogs, and in sporting of every kind, he found no inconsiderable degree of domestic felicity.

For Marianne, however—in spite of his incivility in surviving her loss—he always retained that decided regard which interested him in everything that befell her, and made her his secret standard of perfection in woman; and many a rising beauty would be slighted by him in after days as bearing no comparison with Mrs. Brandon.

Mrs. Dashwood was prudent enough to remain

at the cottage, without attempting a removal to Delaford; and fortunately for Sir John and Mrs. Jennings, when Marianne was taken from them, Margaret had reached an age highly suitable for dancing, and not very ineligible for being supposed to have a lover.

Between Barton and Delaford there was that constant communication which strong family affection would naturally dictate; and among the merits and the happiness of Elinor and Marianne, let it not be ranked as the least considerable that, though sisters, and living almost within sight of each other, they could live without disagreement between themselves, or producing coolness between their husbands.

Printed by T. and A. CONSTABLE, Printers to Her Majesty
at the Edinburgh University Press

www.ingramcontent.com/pod-product-compliance
Lightning Source LLC
Chambersburg PA
CBHW020855020726
47497CB00005B/1416